GW00401266

PART ONE

NEC IN ARCADIA EGO

This book is dedicated to my mother

Muses, what was its fashion, shown
By the skill in all arts
Of the hands of Hephaestus and Athena?
Of bronze the walls, and of bronze
Stood the pillars beneath,
But of gold were six Enchantresses
Who sang above the eagle.
But the sons of Cronus
Opened the earth with a thunderbolt
And hid the holiest of all things made.

Pindar, Paean 8.65-71, translated by C M Bowra

1

For a moment it was perfect: the sun, the shadow, the scent of jasmine winding its way around the window. She could have lain there forever, not even reading, not even thinking, just being.

But already it was time for Jayne to make her way down to the tiny harbour, dotted with boats and reeking of seaweed, to meet her cousins for drinks and dinner.

All things considered she was glad she had taken their suggestion of a holiday together. She had forgotten in the intervening years that they were what her father had described as "boat people": sailing fanatics. Casting her mind back now she remembered a childhood holiday of yellow sou'westers, foul weather and the misery of endlessly tacking around the Isle of Wight in a bitter gale. Since then most shared family occasions had been Easter or Christmas parties and a couple of weddings and funerals.

If her cousins were disappointed by her choice to spend her days on land while they sailed, they put on a cheerful front. And really, spending evenings with them was enough. Jayne was used to her own company. She liked tranquillity. There was plenty to explore. And the peace of the villa with its small, walled garden - more of a courtyard really - enclosed and private and quiet during the day.

They had ended up dining at the same taverna most evenings. Most of the restaurants and bars were alike: ouzo at sunset, the aroma of grilled souvlaki, syrup-oozing baklava. Despite her inertia Jayne was hungry.

She arrived before her cousins and sat contentedly at a table, the same table as the previous night, watching the water. She had been gazing at a small group of divers mooring and preparing to leave their boat some distance away, when she realised one of them looked familiar.

Caroline! She hadn't seen her for several years. One of her set at university, part of a group that shared tutorials and swapped lecture notes, roomed together and socialised together. They had been quite a gang but Jayne had drifted away back to home life after graduation and not kept in touch very well.

And here she was in Greece, slightly surprisingly the only woman in a group of men, all of whom looked Greek or Mediterranean. Jayne didn't remember Caroline having an interest in diving. Something about the group struck her as professional or commercial - they didn't appear to be returning from a leisure dive. It was unusual.

The group were still too far to call out to, so Jayne waited until they had reached the harbour's edge and were a few yards from passing her table. She waved and called out "Caroline!" but the woman in the group didn't respond or even turn her head. "Hi, Caroline!" Jayne called again, but she walked straight past.

Had she been mistaken? She was sure she had not been. Yet something prevented Jayne from running after her. If Caroline was staying here there was a chance of seeing her again even though her holiday was nearing its end. Perhaps she was tired and just wanted to get back to her accommodation and change. Or maybe divers wore some kind of earplugs, Jayne wondered.

Before she could think too much about it her cousins arrived, salt-sprayed and full of enthusiasm for the sea and the sailing. "You really are missing out Jayne," the youngest said. "A great shame you've lost your sea legs." They began an animated discussion about something to do with boats that was beyond Jayne's knowledge or interest, though they cheerfully and obliviously tried to include her, and she smiled and murmured at appropriate moments as the wine came, her mind cast back to her university days.

Et in Arcadia ego. Had it really been only a few years ago? It seemed a distant memory. The relentless roll of the terms, exams, finals. For a time that had been so intense it was odd to find it now such a blur. Had she deliberately buried the memories? The eight of them had seen one another nearly daily for three years but Jayne had barely kept in contact since.

Caroline, long dark brown hair, slightly horsey, kind, hard working. Very bright. From a very different background to Jayne: a titled family with a stately home, but always approachable and without airs. Jayne had very little idea of what had happened to her since they graduated. She knew that Caroline did something in the

3

city at a merchant bank, but she had no idea what precisely. Caroline likely didn't need to work but she was the kind of person who would have done so anyway.

Jayne hadn't gone up to London and embarked on an impressive career like the others. She attributed this to the loss of her parents and the distance from her home town. But was there a faint sense of shame and embarrassment, that she had gone back and done nothing much with her education and rather stagnated. Up until this moment Jayne had thought she was quite happy to stagnate. Now, seeing Caroline again, she felt a sudden sense of loss. What were they all doing? What were their lives like? Were they happy? Did they see one another regularly?

"You're away with the clouds tonight, Jayne," her female cousin, the middle one, said.

Jayne blushed and apologised.

"I thought I saw someone I knew from university, but I didn't manage to catch her attention," she said. "It started me reminiscing."

"It's such a small place here, you'll probably bump into her again," her oldest cousin said.

Yet as he said this Jayne suddenly knew, with a clear and strange premonition, that she wouldn't. If she saw Caroline again it wouldn't be here. She knew within herself that Caroline had heard her, must have seen her. But she had chosen not to respond. She would avoid a future encounter. Despite this Jayne did not feel slighted. She knew that Caroline had good manners and there was no animosity between them. Caroline had no reason to snub her. Whatever her reasons, they had prevented her from being able to stop and make contact, and one day Jayne might well find out why. Jayne was too patient to be very curious but her mind lingered on a few possibilities.

"I don't expect so," Jayne said. "But we'll see."

Thankfully the conversation turned away from sailing to old family anecdotes and Jayne found herself better absorbed in it, insulated from her own thoughts. They were kind people, her cousins, and good company.

"We should take a day off the water and visit Delphi tomorrow," her female cousin was saying.

Her brothers cried her down. "What about our plans to sail to that little island? It's only reachable by water."

"We could always go next week. Or you boys can go without me. I'd like to spend a day here. And poor Jayne, she must be feeling a bit neglected. She's been spending nearly the entire holiday alone."

Jayne wasn't feeling neglected at all but she was touched by her cousin's consideration. She happily agreed to a day of sightseeing and souvenir shopping.

The four cousins walked back to the villa in the inky darkness. There was no moon that night and the narrow streets climbing the hillside were barely lit. The night was close about them; Jayne felt that she could feel it on her skin. A night for mosquitoes, she thought, and made a note to burn some citronella.

The ascent to Delphi mid-morning, after the rickety bus had dropped them at the foot of the site, was idyllic. Yellow broom shone bright in the sunlight as they made their way past ruined shrines and temples to the stadium at the top. It was pleasant to have someone to share it with. Her cousin chatted on about her job and her colleagues and a recent boyfriend she had, and Jayne realised how bare her own life was of people her own age. It really hadn't been since university that she had conversed like this.

Of course Jayne's isolation wasn't entirely her own fault. She had chosen to nurse her father unto the end, anything else was unthinkable to her. He had been a widower, her mother having died several years previously. He was already an elderly man and Jayne was all he had. Family members and neighbours had been very kind but it was her burden.

And then finally he had died. Peacefully and in line with doctors' predictions. There was sadness, deep sadness, but no shock. And Jayne's living situation was unaffected. Her parents, cautious and modest living their whole lives, had left her the house as well as a small income from their careful investments.

So Jayne had stayed at home and drifted for the past few years, tending to the garden that was her parents' pride, involving herself with occasional village events. She wasn't even waiting for something to happen, life just continued. And then this Easter her cousins had invited her over and suggested the holiday. That was the first disruption. And now she had seen Caroline and she rather felt that everything had further shifted and changed. It was time for something new, but she didn't know what.

A couple of thousand years ago she could have consulted the oracle at the very temple she stood before now. "I'm surprised some Greek doesn't dress up in a robe and do predictions for a few drachma. He'd make a mint," her cousin said.

"I think it was a woman actually, the Pythia," Jayne said, consulting her guidebook. "What do you think you would ask an oracle?"

"I don't think you asked them anything specific, they'd just tell you what will be," her cousin said.

What will be. Standing here on this hillside, Mount Parnassus looming to the north. The hum of crickets, the sweet bright scent of broom. I will go home and England will be greyer, thought Jayne. She considered for a moment that she could stay here longer for a few more weeks or even months. She had no commitments and sufficient means.

But winter would come here too.

"You're very pensive, Jayne."

"It's so lovely here, I wondered for a moment about staying on."

"Lucky you! When I think of all my work piling up back in the office."

"Oh, I wasn't really serious," Jayne said. "I need to get back too."

But she didn't, not really. There was no one waiting for her, not even a cat. The garden would cope with a little neglect now summer was ending. Nonetheless she would go back. She wanted to go back. She wanted to try and reconnect with some of the people she'd lost touch with. Even Caroline.

2

So she would not see Caroline again. As the first earth was cast, they stood huddled together a little awkwardly a short distance from the family.

"Christ I hate funerals," Cade said. "I wish they would do private burials. It can't make it any easier for them, having us all here. They don't even know us."

Francis Cade. Now Cade Chetwynd, aspiring actor. He had taken the name from one of their professors, more for the alliteration than the tribute.

It was Cade who had rung her, soon after she had arrived home, to tell her the news. Caroline had been killed in a diving accident. No more than a day after Jayne had seen her, from what she could work out. So unexpected and so terribly sad.

They watched as dark-clad figures, blurred with grief, were led away. No one should outlive their own child.

"I suppose we'd better head to the wake. Do you think we should give it another twenty minutes or so, or would they prefer we arrived as soon as possible and got it over with?"

It was the worst place for a reunion. But they stood together, six of the eight. Alongside Jayne and Cade there was John Lambert, the son of a prominent barrister, practically called to the bar from his cradle and already showing signs of his father's brilliance. Amanda Charles, very bright, forthright and a first class hockey player, currently worked in Westminster. Lucy Easterby-Jones, the ingénue of the group, was employed by a leading auction house. And finally Aubrey Fellowes, antiques lover and aesthete, who produced Arts programming for the BBC. Aubrey's waistcoat and cravat were the most sombre Jayne had ever seen him wear.

The only person missing was Rory Ellis, a former rugby blue, who now worked for an international energy company. He hadn't been able to make it as he was overseas as usual.

They had all done so well and she had done nothing.

Jayne found herself standing with Cade again. She had always been closest to him and he was the only one she'd stayed in touch with to some extent. He sent her theatre bills every so often and invitations to London.

"That's the brother," Cade said, indicating a young man with a round face and rather floppy hair. He was surprisingly tall, his face looked as though it would be better matched with a shorter figure.

"He's Harry, isn't he?" she said, remembering Caroline talking of her family.

"You were always brilliant with names. Go on, see if you can guess her name." Cade pointed to a thin, dark haired girl, rather pretty in a pointy-faced way, standing near Harry. "I heard her introduce herself earlier. You can have a clue. It starts with V."

"Oh, Cade, I honestly wouldn't know," Jayne said. Her gift with names had become something of an in-joke, after a party game where she had matched names to faces with surprising accuracy. It was mainly luck, she thought.

Yet she found herself mulling over the possibilities. "Not a Venetia. Definitely not a Virginia. Probably not a Veronica. A Verity, perhaps, or a Victoria. Not a Vivienne." She rather hoped it wasn't Verity. It was a name she liked and somehow she did not like the look of this girl.

Cade raised his eyebrows. "You really are good. It's Victoria. Goodness, I wonder who that is. I didn't see him at the burial."

Caroline looked over to an even taller man than Harry, blond, with strikingly attractive looks. "That might be the cousin, though I can't remember his name. I do remember she had a cousin she was very fond of." More of a hero-worship in fact, though seeing him now Jayne could hardly blame Caroline for her cousinly adoration. Poor Caroline.

"If it only was possible to sever Victoria from him," Cade said. "He's far too beautiful to be wasted on her. She's his fiancée, from what I overheard."

"I imagine she would be a more than considerable obstacle then," said Jayne. "Besides which, how could you be sure if he..."

"If he's keen to bat for the Chetwynd Eleven?" Cade said. "Perhaps not. You'd be surprised though."

"We should have been meeting at a wedding, not a wake," Lucy said.

The six of them had gone to a local pub afterwards though no one felt like eating much. It was a long drive back to London, longer for Jayne with her train journey ahead, and being Saturday there was scant impetus to hurry back.

"Jayne saw Caroline in Greece, you know," Cade said. When he had phoned to give her the news, her first reaction was to try and deny it, to tell him that she'd only recently seen Caroline, that she couldn't possibly be dead.

"I didn't get a chance to speak to her though, I only saw her from a distance," Jayne said, fibbing slightly. She didn't want to open speculation as to whether Caroline had deliberately blanked her or not, or had water in her ears from diving. "I very much regret that I didn't manage to meet her again. It was near the end of my holiday and I had no idea where she was staying."

Cade turned to her. "I thought you only came back a few days ago?"

"Yes, that's right, it was the previous weekend, she was by the harbour. Such a small world."

There was a very uncomfortable silence.

"Jayne, Caroline was killed three weeks ago," Cade said.

"But she couldn't have been," Jayne said automatically, without thinking. "It was on the seventh that I saw her."

"She died on the first," Lucy said. "It was on the order of service. Harry flew out there immediately afterwards to deal with all the official things and make the arrangements."

11

Edward Turbeville

Jayne was flustered. Something must be very wrong, or she was losing her mind. But now was not the time.

"Of course, I am sorry, I'm hopeless with dates. I have all my weeks mixed up."

There was a show of sympathetic understanding but Jayne could feel Cade's eyes intent upon her as she looked miserably into her drink, her thoughts in turmoil. She felt she had embarrassed herself and somehow injured Caroline's memory. And yet she was quite certain of the date. It could easily be verified through the records of her booking arrangements or by her cousins.

For now the awkwardness dulled the enormity of the realisation. They moved onto other topics but the mood had started miserably and had only become worse now, so they parted ways soon afterwards.

Cade didn't drive and had declined a lift, choosing to take a train back despite the extra expense. He claimed he liked train journeys but Jayne knew that he wanted to question her. He knew her better than any of the others did, more than the girls even, though she and Amanda had been quite close once.

Cade bought his ticket and came to sit with her on the platform as they would be taking the same train for the first part of the journey.

"You see it looked like it could have been a seven, the writing was rather Italic, either that or I assumed it was a misprint," Jayne began.

"What are you talking about?"

"The date on the programme. I thought it was a seven. Obviously it was a one. Now I don't know what to think."

Cade spoke firmly. "Jayne, did you or did you not see Caroline alive on the seventh? Forget the programme, do you think that you saw Caroline the Saturday before last, not three weeks ago?"

"I don't think it, I did see her," Jayne said. "But of course I can't have done, can I?"

"There are only two explanations, or three, but I think we can discount Banquo's ghost. Either you were mistaken and saw someone that looked like Caroline, or you did see her and the date of death is wrong. Given that she didn't answer, the obvious thing is that you made a mistake and it was a total stranger. But I know you, you're precise and you're good with faces. So the theory I have is that you actually saw Caroline a week or so earlier, perhaps in a crowd, and forgot about it. Then a slightly similar woman triggered your memory and somehow got superimposed with Caroline in your mind."

It sounded plausible enough.

"The others must think I'm such an idiot, so crass," Jayne said.

"Not at all. We were all shocked by her death. Coming back from holiday, with different time zones and things, anybody can get confused."

Train journeys were never the enjoyment that Jayne always imagined, remembering old films, with porters and private carriages and hatboxes. She sat across a scratched plastic table from Cade, there were newspapers and empty cups and sandwich wrappings strewn all over the place. A horrid grimy little window curtain was tied back with string, its clasp broken.

"You must come up and see my new play," Cade said. "It's quite fun. I'll send you tickets."

"I'd love to, thank you."

"You've been hibernating far too long. We've all been remiss. Let's make this a new start and keep in touch properly from now on. You're always welcome to stay."

Jayne smiled. "I've missed you, Cade. I'm sorry I haven't been there. I know we all promised to see every single one of your performances."

"Well, that was perhaps a promise too far. It's forgiven. But you'll come up and lunch with Aubrey and I. We'll reminisce. Drown ourselves in wine and nostalgia."

The train drew up at the station where Jayne had to change, and they parted ways.

3

The garden was lovely in late summer, and easier to manage. There were fewer weeds yet no leaves to rake yet. It had been her parents' joy: a winding maze of trellised roses, espaliered fruit trees, a knot garden of kitchen herbs that was both beautiful and useful. Jayne felt a pang of bitterness that they could no longer enjoy it.

She sat for a moment in the late afternoon sun on the small bench where her mother had liked to read. She closed her eyes, but then became aware of someone else arriving in the strange unconscious way that feels like a sixth sense.

Opening her eyes she was startled to see the tall blond man from Caroline's funeral approaching.

"I beg your pardon, there was no answer at the front door, but I saw the side gate open."

He had a calm and pleasant voice. "I saw you at Caroline's funeral, though we didn't speak," he continued. "My name is Lucas. I'm Caroline and Harry's cousin."

"Caroline mentioned you many times." Her eyes held her sympathy.

"I should explain why I have come. I apologise for not managing to telephone you in advance."

Jayne urged him to accept a drink first, and he chose to stay outside rather than accompany her indoors. He mentioned the loveliness of the garden and the afternoon, delaying the explanation for his visit.

Inside she was able to glance in a mirror, fearing a stray leaf in her hair or smudge on her face, but there was nothing to be embarrassed by. She was glad of the high brick walls that guarded against neighbourly curiosity, for the elderly woman next door kept a keen eye on other people's comings and goings and a gentleman caller would greatly have piqued her interest.

Lucas was sitting on the small bench when she came out, but he immediately rose when he saw her, thanking her for the drink. After they had sat down again he spoke.

"The reason I came is because I feel a sort of duty. Caroline was like a little sister to me. Someone mentioned that you had seen her in Greece shortly before she died and I just wondered..." He tailed off.

"Lucas, I'm so terribly sorry, it seems that I made a mistake. The woman I saw, well she can't have been Caroline because it was after she died. Of course I didn't know at the time, and I became a little muddled with the dates."

He looked disappointed. "Thank you anyway. It did seem a strange coincidence."

"Yes, for us to both have been there at the same time but not have met up, I'll always regret it. Cade - our friend Francis Cade - he wondered if I had actually glimpsed

Caroline a week or so before, and remembered that instead. And then perhaps confused her with a similar looking woman. I'm so sorry I don't have anything more to tell you, and that you've wasted your journey."

Lucas was silent for a moment. "This woman, you were absolutely sure that she looked like Caroline?"

"Well yes, I mean I thought it was Caroline. Not even that she merely resembled her. But obviously it couldn't have been."

"You didn't even doubt?"

Jayne wasn't sure where he was heading or how to respond. She felt miserably embarrassed about the whole affair. "No. I actually called out to her and she didn't respond. Which of course she wouldn't have, she wouldn't have known me at all since she couldn't have been Caroline."

"How close were you, I mean the distance?"

"Perhaps a couple of yards, at the nearest."

He looked at her intently, dark grey eyes meeting hers, and Jayne suddenly realised that he believed her. He believed as much, perhaps more, than she did that she had seen Caroline. For a moment she felt exultation, a strange thrill after days of feeling excruciating embarrassment and increasing self-doubt.

Then he spoke.

"I am not satisfied with my cousin's death. I think - I feel certain - that she is dead, or we would have heard something from her by now. But I am not satisfied that it was an accident. Caroline was a very sensible girl. But lately she may have been mixed up in something unusual."

"But her brother - Harry - he flew over and oversaw everything, surely?"

"I don't believe Harry ever saw the body. He's squeamish. He wouldn't even visit our grandmother when she was dying."

None of it made sense. And yet anything felt more believable than the accepted events, *because she had seen Caroline.*

"What would you like me to do?" She knew without him asking that he had a request to make of her.

"I want to find out more about Caroline's life before she died. What she was doing, whom she was with. And if there are any irregularities. I don't trust the police in a place like Greece. They can easily be bought. There are some lines of enquiry I plan to follow up, but we share a surname and it is an uncommon surname. My concern is that it will deprive me of the opportunity of casually discovering information. If I am immediately identified as a member of the family it may close doors or cause complications."

Jayne made it easy for him. "Would you like me to go back to Greece and have a look around?"

His face lit up for a moment. "It's a lot to ask, I know. But you have been there already and you were the one who saw her. I would greatly appreciate a partner in this, an ally. The family could also be upset if they found out I was investigating."

He means Harry, thought Jayne. He's the one who will be blamed if there has been a mix up. She shivered for a moment. Someone else's bones may lie in Caroline's grave if Harry had failed to properly view the body. But whose were they?

"We'll go to dinner," Lucas told her. "Please do me and Caroline the honour of being my guest. We'll sit and drink to her and plan our quest. I can't lay her to rest, in my own mind, until I have made this final attempt for her."

And so they had become a team. As they left the garden to go to Lucas's car Jayne felt a sudden sadness. A chapter in her life was closing forever, and an unknown one beginning.

4

It was glorious lunching with Cade and Aubrey. It brought her straight back to their university days. Jayne hadn't realised how much she'd missed them. She had first hoped that Lucy might join them but Cade didn't suggest it, and it was easier with just the three of them. Aubrey's eccentricity had mellowed and sat more comfortably upon him as the years had passed.

She didn't tell them anything about Lucas or Caroline. It was too complicated. And she wanted to enjoy this treat, this last bask in the past, as though the past four years had been rolled away and they had no cares except an essay deadline or cramming for an exam.

Aubrey brushed crumbs from his plum-coloured waistcoat.

"I understand that our thespian colleague is attempting to prise you from a life of spinsterhood and jam-making in the depths of Little Mumblebury."

Jayne laughed. "I have spent a rather quiet couple of years but I'm not about to marry the curate, if that's your concern."

"A shame. I like jam," Aubrey said.

"Tell me about what you've been up to. Did you find anything interesting on your latest trip?" Jayne asked him. Aubrey's antique collecting frequently took him across the country as well as abroad. He had most recently been to Scotland.

"Haggis, foul weather, and tartan-painted Chippendale. Or it may as well have been, for all it had any beauty or value."

"And you're still making it big in broadcasting, Cade tells me?"

"One tries. One endeavours to elevate this fair land from the mire of crass tawdriness into which it hurls itself headlong." Aubrey sighed.

"A graveyard chat on the wireless about a few sculptures and vases is hardly the next renaissance," Cade said. "Theatre, on the other hand..."

"No," interrupted Aubrey. "And no again. I have now sat through two performances of your excruciating show and I will not endure it thrice. Not even to accompany Jayne." Cade had given her tickets to see his play that night.

"It can't be that bad?" Jayne asked.

"You'll adore it," Aubrey told her. "It's quite brilliant, quite dazzling, yet it strangles my soul. Besides, I have a prior engagement. No, not a date. An aunt. An elderly maiden aunt of sizeable means and generous disposition. We shall dine at Claridges, for she finds The Ritz intolerable." He reached for another roll. "Now, tell me about your ghost."

Jayne was taken aback. "My ghost?"

"The ghost of our poor friend Caroline. Whom, or which - is a ghost a person or an object? - I understand you saw in Greece. Such phenomena fascinate me."

"It wasn't anything of the kind, just an awkward misunderstanding." There was no need to mention Lucas and her planned return trip.

"A mysterious girl, poor Caroline," Aubrey continued his theme. "Not quite all she seemed, I have long suspected."

Food arrived, diverting his attention away as suddenly as it had turned to the subject.

They didn't speak of Caroline again. Nor did they even reminisce about the old times. Conversation moved to topical issues, politics and scandals in the theatre and media worlds that Cade and Aubrey worked in. Even when they spoke of people she didn't know, they were entertaining. Jayne was surprised how quickly she fell back into their old rhythm. She had usually been the listener of the group, their audience. And now she was so again.

Cade's play was indeed entertaining. Jayne had been fearful of enduring something overly highbrow. But it was an enjoyable, contemporary thriller. Unlike previous shows that Cade had made her sit through, there were no lengthy speeches in Bosnian or naked actors sitting in cages from curtain up to encore, representing some concept that Jayne didn't care to even try and understand.

Cade had at least been among the clothed cast members in that production.

He met her outside the stage door. "Well?"

"I liked it very much."

"Did you? I'm always rather disappointed by the motive. I'm sure I should have killed for revenge or some bizarre sexual deviancy, not money," Cade said. "I've been tempted to change it, perhaps at the end of a matinée, by which time the audience will all be asleep anyway."

"You may upset the writer," Jayne said.

"Most probably. Besides which, in practice people only ever really kill for money."

"Do they?"

"They claim it's jealousy, or passion, but it's always about their own wealth and status or not letting the ex-wife get the house. At least that's what John Lambert says, and he should know," Cade told her. Like his renowned father, John practised criminal law.

"I always expected John and Lucy would be our first wedding. I'm surprised things haven't moved along more quickly there."

"I'm not," said Cade. "He's too ambitious, and she's too sweet."

They had walked to a small bistro that opened into the early hours and usually thronged with theatre folk. After the waiter took their order, Jayne asked Cade something that had been in her mind since lunch.

"What Aubrey said earlier about Caroline being mysterious. Did he really mean anything by that, or was he just being Aubrey?"

"It's always hard to tell with Aubrey," Cade said, avoiding a reply.

"Caroline always seemed to straightforward to me. So down-to-earth." Jayne frowned. How was she going to return to Greece and seek for Caroline's ghost, so to speak, when she wasn't really sure who her old friend was anymore?

Cade was silent for a short while, twisting a napkin. "I never mentioned anything before, because, well it never really needed to come up. And I'm not certain it even does now, really. But I'm pretty sure Caroline received The Summons," he said.

"The Summons?"

"MI5 or MI6, whatever it is."

"Cade, are you being absurd?"

"Not at all. You must have heard of it happening to people, rumours at least?" Jayne hadn't. "Well, this is according to someone's brother's friend's barber's dog, so make of it what you will. You remember going to one for those informal career chats with your tutor before Finals?"

Jayne did, and rather sadly. Explaining how her only real plans were to return and care for an elderly parent, and feeling there was disappointment mixed with the sympathy returned to her.

"If you're not really set on any path, and they think you might be suitable, or useful, perhaps," Cade continued. "Apparently they suggest you might like to go and pay a visit to Professor Plum at St Bungles or whatever, and then he tips you the wink and does the funny handshake and you're signed and sealed and Secret Service."

Three weeks ago Jayne might have protested the likelihood of this happening to Caroline. Now it seemed as though it might be an important piece of the puzzle.

"How do you know?" she asked.

"About Caroline? It was something someone said once, just a throwaway remark. I forgot about it for ages. It was only when you said she was in Greece in such odd sounding company that I wondered. But of course you didn't see her, did you? Or probably you didn't."

If she was ever going to tell him, now was the time. He was her closest friend and Lucas hadn't sworn her to secrecy, albeit discretion was assumed. But she could trust Cade.

"I had a visitor the other day," she began. And she told him what Lucas had said, and what he had asked of her.

It took Cade a while to digest. "First, I should say that I'm both impressed and envious about the cousin. Secondly, none of this makes any sense at all. Why wouldn't he just hire a private investigation agent? He must be rolling in it."

"Perhaps he will," Jayne said. "I think since I'd been there he thought I could more easily retrace her steps."

"I suspect a more personal interest." Cade looked pointedly at her.

"Don't be ridiculous! Besides which he's engaged to be married."

Cade dismissed this fact with a gesture.

"Jayne, you are very beautiful. No - don't protest. I always said you should have gone onto the stage too."

"I can't act for toffee."

"Those green-amber eyes and dark honey hair," Cade continued, taking a strand of her hair analytically. "But you have no self-awareness. You could have had Rory eating out of your hand but you were far too passive. All those silly Sloanes rushing to launder his rugger kit and tossing their hair about. You never stood a chance against them, just sitting there silently longing."

This was painful to hear. For most of her time at university Jayne had had a fondness for Rory, who now worked overseas. But she had never managed to articulate it to him.

"How is Rory doing now, do you know?" she asked.

"The same as ever. Too rugged for his own good, charging around in dangerous locations for various mining companies. I should think you would find you had outgrown him," Cade said.

He stood up. "Anyway, onto bigger and better things. Would you like to go on to a club, or shall we head home?"

Jayne chose the latter. Cade had rattled her and her thoughts were whirling, and she wanted the numbness of sleep.

5

Lucas had asked to meet her for lunch while she was still in London. Jayne assumed it was to discuss details of her return trip to Greece, so she was rather disconcerted when his fiancée Victoria and Caroline's brother Harry joined them as well.

She had been right about Victoria too, she thought, as she observed the other woman's behaviour throughout the meal. Despite her engagement she seemed to be making a play for Harry. Rather crudely too, though Harry seemed oblivious. She also exhibited oddly competitive behaviour towards Jayne. Victoria's strategy involved ignoring her as far as possible, making slights and digs where she could, and showing exaggerated interest and approval in anything Harry said or did.

Jayne wondered if Lucas noticed. She fancied he did but if so he didn't appear to be bothered by it. She looked from him to Harry. The latter's round, cheery face bore a strong resemblance to Caroline. But, strangely, he didn't remind Jayne of her, whereas Lucas did.

Near strangers whose only real connection to you is a bereavement do not make the easiest lunch companions. But Lucas showed surprising skill at managing the conversation. He was someone who naturally took command of a situation. Jayne sensed Harry resented this. He made several flippant remarks that verged on petulance. By himself Harry seems a man, thought Jayne, but next to Lucas he appears juvenile. Why on earth was Victoria making up to him?

"So what do you do, Jayne?" Victoria asked. It should have been an innocent enough question yet Jayne suspected that Victoria already knew that Jayne didn't really do anything at the moment. Victoria herself worked at a gallery, but her lack of interest and knowledge of art, apparent as conversation touched on the subject, marked her as a dabbler rather than a careerist. A little token job before she marries money, Jayne thought uncharitably. She hoped for his sake that Lucas had plenty.

"Caroline had some very interesting plans for the house," Lucas said. "Do you intend to continue with any of them?"

According to Lucas, Caroline had planned to turn a wing of the house into a convalescent retreat. She also had some innovative ideas for the grounds. The hefty upkeep of the house necessitated it generating some kind of revenue, and Caroline and Harry's parents had done little beyond opening it up to tour groups in summer.

"I think that's a private family issue," Harry said.

Jayne felt uncomfortable, knowing she was the only non-family member there. Victoria enjoyed official status thanks to the ring on her finger, an heirloom of emeralds and diamond, which she made a point of playing with at that moment.

"We spent a lot of time at the house together as children, back when our grandparents were still alive. But it's challenging to maintain. Even the National Trust won't take on many homes these days," Lucas explained for Jayne's benefit.

"I assure you the house will be amply maintained," Harry said, a haughty edge to his voice.

"Harry's always had lots of ideas about the house," Victoria said, defending him. "I'm sure he'll do something very clever."

"I never doubted it," Lucas said. To change the mood he hailed a waiter and ordered coffees, though Harry still seemed to be sulking.

Later Jayne and Lucas walked through a nearby park. Victoria had to return to work, and contrived to have Harry escort her, since he was headed in the same direction. Jayne felt a great gladness and relief that they were gone.

"I'm afraid I rub Harry up the wrong way," Lucas said. "But I wanted you to meet him properly before you go."

Jayne had suspected as much. She also had the strong impression that Lucas had not told Victoria about their investigation, nor even mentioned his visit to her. Since she couldn't think of a way to broach this, she left it hanging. Perhaps it didn't matter. It was Lucas's prerogative either way.

"I'm anxious I won't be able to get you any answers," she said. "There is one thing though." She told him what Cade had heard.

"Yes, I knew," Lucas said. "Caroline didn't tell me directly but it was clear. That's why I need to establish whether her death was really an accident. She deserves that."

They sat in silence, watching the ducks. Summer is starting to fade, Jayne thought. Who will clear the leaves when I'm away?

She wondered how long she would need to stay overseas for. Lucas had instructed her to send all her expenses to him, but she wasn't comfortable about doing so. If she failed, it would feel like accepting payment for a job undone. Instead she resolved to live by her own means as far as possible. In a way this was her quest too.

Lucas spoke, interrupting her thoughts.

"There was a boy at school whose father worked behind the Iron Curtain, and provided intelligence to Britain. The Soviets got wind. They came to his office and threw him out of the window."

Jayne was horrified.

Lucas continued. "This man did what he did out of loyalty, patriotism, call it what you will. He wasn't even paid. After his murder, it was reported back home that he was an alcoholic, and had jumped while drunk from the twentieth storey. They do what they need to suit their own ends, regardless of any additional pain caused to the bereaved."

"You mean that Caroline might have died on the job, rather than accidentally?"

"Easily. Certainly, I should say. But the timing still doesn't make sense." Lucas had been looking across the park, but now he turned to face her.

"Let me articulate what we need to confront. It is possible that Caroline faked her own death. If so, it is then possible she is still alive. But given the length of time that has elapsed, I have minimal hope of this. If Caroline had switched allegiance, as has happened, she would be safely behind the Iron Curtain by now, and word would have been sent.

"If she had been playing some dangerous game, faking her own death, she might have brought the risk upon herself. It's easier to be killed if you're already considered dead. No one comes looking for you."

"You base a lot of faith in my fleeting glimpse of her."

"You saw her, relatively close up, in a location where we now have proof she was. You had no reason to be thinking of her, or looking for her. You were absolutely convinced that you saw Caroline, to the point of never seriously considering that it might have been someone who looked like her. On this point, Caroline was not Greek, and the chances of someone closely resembling her, unlikely enough even here in London, would be even less over there."

He stood up.

"We also know that her life was complex. On balance, I consider that there are more reasons to find it credible that you did see her, than to think that you were mistaken."

Before Jayne left for Greece again she met with Amanda, Lucy and John for coffee. Rory was still overseas. Jayne was rather disappointed by John's presence in their company, as it inhibited the conversation that the three women might have had otherwise. John was so serious and stuffy. Cade was right, Jayne found herself struggling to imagine what chemistry existed between him and Lucy. They certainly weren't very demonstrative in public.

"Aubrey tells me you're going back to Greece," Amanda said.

"Yes. It's actually at the request of Caroline's cousin. He was dissatisfied with some of the details of her death, and thought that I may be of use, having already been there. I am not sure that there's much I can do, but for Caroline's sake I didn't like to refuse."

"You are lucky just being able to up sticks and flit off whenever you please," Lucy said.

"Yes, I suppose I am." Though she would give it all up to have her parents back, Jayne thought, since it was only their deaths that had enabled her leisure. But she said nothing.

"Had there been any questions over the death, an inquest would have been held here," John said. "A wiser course of action, if the relatives are genuinely concerned, would be to engage a local lawyer or inquiry agent."

"I will suggest it," Jayne said. She found something irritatingly arrogant in John's tone. It was his area of law, of course, but he needled her. She wished again it could have been just the three of them.

"Is it easy to get by there, without speaking Greek?" Amanda asked.

"It's a busy area for tourism, so one can be quite lazy and rely on English from dawn to dusk. At least in the main sightseeing areas, and bars and restaurants."

"I've always wanted to see the Greek isles," Lucy said. She looked rather wistful.

"Where I'm staying is actually on the mainland, by the Gulf of Corinth. Quite far from the Aegean," Jayne told her. "It's still very beautiful though."

6

Greece was exactly as she had left it. It was still summer on the Corinthian coast. Autumn would take its time to arrive.

Jayne was not staying in the hillside villa this time. She had briefly considered it, but it was aimed at holiday rentals for larger groups and was rather out of the way. Instead she found a tiny house in the town, the Villa Kallina, located through a labyrinth of narrow streets. She struggled to remember landmarks along the route; she knew it would be very difficult to find her way back after dark.

"Turn at the lemon tree, second street on the left, right after the niche with flowers, round the house with blue shutters, then left again," she memorised.

The house was divided into two sections, and Jayne had the lower rooms. The kitchen was a cool, cellar-like chamber, and she was grateful for the protection of its thick walls against the heat, still a force to be reckoned with in late August. Unlike the villa there was no air conditioning here, nor ceiling fans.

Though she was anxious about getting lost in the winding alleys at night, Jayne did not want to waste any time. She started out at the same taverna from where she had seen Caroline. It seemed smaller than before, the distance from the harbour's edge to her table even closer. Jayne watched other people walking past. She could see their faces clearly with good detail. As she had correctly remembered, the table was only a few yards away from passers-by.

The waiters at this particular establishment were far less garrulous than at other places, which was partly why she and her cousins had tended to frequent it, preferring to dine in peace. This was no longer ideal for Jayne's purpose. She needed people who would strike up a conversation and be happy to gossip. So after her meal she walked along the waterfront and entered a popular bar, called the Apollo.

Back in England sitting by herself in a pub and ordering drinks would have felt excruciating. As a single woman on holiday it seemed much easier. Waiters were more eager to chat and flatter. One in particular struck Jayne as worth cultivating: a young Greek man with dark hair curling over his collar, looking in need of a haircut compared to the other staff. But his English was nearly fluent.

Jayne had decided to bite the bullet and disclose having a friend who had died recently, near the town. Unusual or accidental death sparks comment and speculation, and it meant gossip would more likely be offered to her. Whereas seeking it out herself might eventually rouse suspicion. It seemed reasonable enough to explain her trip there as a kind of homage to her friend. It also explained her return to anyone that might have recognised her as being there before.

She struck gold with Yiannis, as he turned out to be called.

"It's so sad," he said. "This girl, your friend, dead, this other missing. It is bad for tourism."

"Someone is missing?"

"Yes, the niece of Spyros, of Spyros Taverna."

Jayne knew where it was, though she had not been there.

"What happened?"

"No one knows. This Maria Tsakalotos, one day she does not appear for work. Dimitris here," a younger waiter passing them flashed a grin, "he goes to help Spyros in his bar for a few days. But now Spyros's younger son is back from Athens."

The younger man, Dimitris, said something in Greek. Yiannis nodded. "He asks if we talk about Maria. I tell him yes."

Dimitris spoke again, at greater length this time, and Jayne thought she caught the words Patras and Delphi.

"She was from Patras, Maria," Yiannis translated. "So it was thought she had gone back there. But no one has seen her. Now the police are investigating."

Translators frequently abridge and Jayne had no reason to think that Yiannis was hiding anything. But she was certain Dimitris had said Delphi, yet Yiannis made no mention of it.

If not a definite lead, Maria's disappearance was a useful topic to break ice with other townspeople. The next day Jayne visited Spyros's establishment. He was a large man, with proficient if heavily accented English, who wrung his hands and gesticulated wildly as he spoke. Usefully he had put up several posters of Maria in his bar. Jayne couldn't read Greek but she assumed the single word at the top must mean "missing" or perhaps "reward". "Mapia" was clearly Maria.

The girl looked to be in her early twenties with long, straight dark hair. "Is this your niece?" Jayne asked him. "Someone mentioned she was missing. I am very sorry."

"She is a nitwit. Two thousand years ago the gods left Delphi. Greeks are not idiots. We do not worship Apollo."

Jayne struggled to understand him. "What's the connection with Delphi?"

"I wish nothing to do with it, I tell you. Na!" he opened out his hand as though to an imaginary presence, extending all five fingers. Jayne had seen Greek drivers do this when coming in opposite directions along too-narrow streets, both refusing to budge. It wasn't a friendly gesture.

"When did she go missing?" Jayne asked.

"After Hekatombaion."

This made little sense to Jayne. "I beg your pardon?"

"The festival last month. Some of them they go on to Delphi. They say it is for Apollo. I say it is for wickedness, drugs."

Jayne remembered that there had been a street party of sorts in the town with a procession. It had taken place around the middle of her holiday. She and her cousins had wondered what it was about at the time. If Maria had gone missing amidst drunken revelry, Jayne couldn't see what connection there was to Caroline.

Except the date. "Spyros, when was Hekatombaion?"

"The end of June of course." He looked at her as though she had asked him when Christmas was.

The same night, then, that Caroline had drowned. It was impossible not to wonder.

Jayne looked again at the photograph of Maria. It was only black and white and a photocopy. She looked nothing like Caroline, to anyone that knew Caroline. But the two were of similar age with long, dark hair. Jayne didn't really want to start thinking about bodies and drowning and features bloating beyond recognition. But it couldn't be ignored.

She telephoned Lucas later, from the villa.

"Nothing much to report so far, just a few unformed thoughts. Given what we discussed before, do you know if they carried out any kind of autopsy? Was it definitely established that Caroline died by drowning, as opposed to being put in the water afterwards? Or perhaps being put there while unconscious? I'm sorry to be so grisly," Jayne said.

"Don't be, they were my first questions too. According to Harry, everything was done by the book." There was something in his voice that Jayne couldn't put her finger on, but the line was crackly.

"Do you mean that the police or whoever might have told Harry that they'd dotted all the i's and crossed the t's, when in fact they hadn't?" she asked.

"That's one possibility."

"So Harry did formally identify the body?"

"I believe so. He certainly signed the official forms."

"The only other thing is there's a girl missing," Jayne said. "And she disappeared the same night that Caroline drowned. I expect it's just a coincidence. A Greek girl who worked in one of the tavernas. Of similar age, with similar hair..."

"You think it's possible there could have been a mix-up?" Lucas asked.

"It was only a very vague thought. If the appearance was altered by drowning, and obviously Harry was suffering from grief and shock, and perhaps wasn't able to take a very close look."

"Yes, it's something to consider. I think it's highly likely he no more than glanced, in all honesty."

Jayne imagined the white sheet being drawn back to reveal a lifeless face. She could understand not wanting to take more than a fleeting glimpse, the grief would already be unbearable without that as well.

She was about to say goodnight, but suddenly remembered another detail. "Lucas, have you heard of Hekatombaion? I believe it's some sort of traditional Greek festival."

"Never, but I'm no Greek scholar. I'll find out for you tomorrow. Sleep well."

7

The next day was cooler and overcast, and as the town seemed to sleep in the daytime Jayne went again to Delphi. Its character was altered by the duller weather. Now it seemed more broken and more rubble-strewn. But the golden broom still added colour as she wended her way up the mountainside.

Most of the other tourists visiting the site seemed to be German. Jayne spoke French and managed a little Italian but German was beyond her scope. This allowed her more peace, since any conversation was rapidly curtailed by language differences. She knew from past travel experiences that a lone voyager often has company thrust upon them, well-meaning but misguided; fortunately that was less likely here.

Now she had arrived at the top she wasn't really sure what to do, and if there had even been any point coming here. Still, gathering her thoughts might be better than nothing. Jayne got out her notebook and feeling slight embarrassment as her skills at botanical drawing were very amateur, began sketching a broom flower.

Physically it was an absorbing, mechanical task, and it allowed her mind to wander. Last night she had suffered horrid dreams of drowning and people with the wrong faces, and twisted faces. Now as she relaxed, she could develop a better perspective on the whole situation.

"If you sweep the house with blossomed broom in May
You are sure to sweep the head of the house away."

How on earth had she remembered that? It was years since she had looked in her parents' old herbals. What odd superstitions people had in olden times. A rhubarb leaf salad or carelessly picked amanita, at any time of year, would far better serve a botanically-inclined murderer than broom flowers.

A murderer. Jayne realised that she no longer even considered it a possibility that Caroline's death had been accidental. Her gut feeling was firmly fixed on unnatural causes.

But what could she really do? She didn't have the knowledge or ability to investigate a murder done at the command of some shadowy faction, maybe even a foreign government. She knew nothing about intelligence or espionage or whatever Caroline had been doing here. It was foolish to have ever come back.

And yet as she sat in this ruined garden of gods and prophets, beneath mighty Parnassus, she felt a sense of purpose. She laid down her pencil and rose. There were three things she could do. She could sit by the harbour each evening and watch to see if the divers ever returned. She would try to find out if anyone had met Caroline and where she had been staying. And for good measure, and because she was not fully confident about success in her first tasks, she would find out everything she could about Maria Tsakalotos.

That afternoon Jayne tried the police. Her goal was to find out exactly where Caroline died, and any details that might establish what she was doing and whom she was with.

The officer on duty was disgruntled at first since Jayne had arrived during the unofficial siesta when he was not inclined to work.

After extensive polite persuasion and the transfer of several hundred drachma, dressed up as "document fees" but patently a bribe, Jayne finally had some useful information. Most of it admittedly was from the officer's personal recollection, but his memory night not have been jogged without the expensive document searches.

Caroline's body had been found off the waters of a small island known as Nisis Lathrémporos. It was impossible to say where she had been diving and no boat had been found. Prevailing currents likely washed her there from the mainland but the police couldn't be certain. Or didn't care, Jayne thought.

Caroline had been staying in a house called the Villa Pythia but had frequently been absent overnight. As such no alarm was raised when she hadn't returned by the morning, and it was a fisherman who finally alerted police to the body, washed up on rocks, later the next day.

Jayne mentioned Maria Tsakalotos but information was not much more forthcoming. She mixed with bad people, the policeman said. But when pushed he wouldn't reveal anything further.

The Villa Pythia was set up on the hillside. It was very similar to the villa that Jayne and her cousins had first stayed at, subdivided into different holiday lettings, with a high white wall and a black-clad landlady who inconveniently did not speak a word of English.

By means of a photo Jayne managed to convey the purpose of her visit. The old woman nodded vigorously in recognition and showed her to the rooms that Caroline had occupied. They had long since been thoroughly cleaned: fresh sheets were tightly tucked in across the twin beds, the small bathroom gleamed. There was no trace of Caroline or any of her belongings. Had Harry taken everything back or had they been thrown away? Jayne had had to sort through the belongings of the deceased twice now, when each of her parents died, and she sent her silent sympathies to Harry.

It was rather a blow. Jayne had somehow felt that finding Caroline's accommodation would throw up some clues, but there was nothing left.

There seemed to be little else that could be achieved here. There was only one other guest left now the holiday season was drawing to a close, and from what Jayne could establish he had only been there a few days.

With sunset approaching, she headed back to the harbourside.

Yiannis was delighted to see her back at the Apollo and insisted on a complimentary ouzo.

"Is there much diving around here?" Jayne asked him.

"Not officially. There are a lot of government restrictions to protect archaeological sites," he said.

"I was wondering more about commercial diving, I saw a group of divers come into the harbour the other day. Are there any companies that you know of?"

Yiannis shrugged. Jayne changed tack. "The girl who is missing, Maria. Several people have said she got into bad company. What do they mean exactly?"

"That I wouldn't know. But usually they mean drugs."

He put a small dish of olives on the bar.

"Probably that she was a part of that idiotic new movement. The Delphinians, they call themselves. Originally they wanted to try and revive old customs and festivals. Now half of them are prophesying the return of Apollo, and the rest are on drugs. They have big parties, so lots of students come from Athens and elsewhere. And weird Bulgarians and others. It's not good for business, when they all go off to the mountain to drink," Yiannis said.

Telephoning Lucas that night felt strangely intimate. He seemed glad to hear from her and the line was much clearer. Jayne reported her progress.

"You've done a lot for less than two days," he said.

"I was disappointed by the Villa Pythia though. I rather felt I'd struck gold there, getting the name from the policeman, but it was a dead end. I suppose I could try finding out about tides, but I don't know if that would narrow the scope much."

"Probably not. By the way I asked a friend about that festival you mentioned. Hekatombaion. It's the first month of the Attic year, or July by today's calendar. Traditionally they sacrificed a hundred cattle to Apollo. By traditionally

I mean very early on - my friend had to go and look it up - it wasn't even celebrated any more by Classical times."

"They've revived it then," Jayne said, and told him about the Delphinians.

"It sounds harmless enough, like a Greek Glastonbury perhaps."

"Yes and with the same substance-taking by all accounts. And Bulgarians!" Jayne included the last remark in humour, but Lucas was silent for a moment.

"This may be starting to make sense," he said finally. "I won't bore you with all the political details, but I have spoken with some people and if Caroline was doing anything out there intelligence-wise, Bulgarian and Yugoslavian terror cells are a key possibility. Please be very careful."

"These Delphinians appear to be just a sort of hippy movement though, not at all political," Jayne said.

"Anything can be a front. Keep your eyes and ears open, and be very careful with your investigations. I'm stuck here for the next couple of days, and there are some more matters I need to look into, but I will try to fly out at the end of the week. Stay safe until then."

Possibilities that had been floating around Jayne's mind were now solidifying. She still couldn't get her head around the timing though. Backdating someone's death was one thing, perhaps to obscure a trail or an official operation, but to announce the death to family even while the person was still alive? It made no sense. What if Harry had bumped into Caroline while dealing with all the formalities? Though if he had, perhaps she would be alive today.

8

It became easy to drift into a regular pattern there, becoming more familiar in the community of young Greeks, backpackers and even a few artists and other travellers. There was a stark contrast between the modern generation and the older Greeks: black clad women sweeping their tiny houses, peasants in the fields, old men twisting worry beads who had never travelled more than five miles from their birthplace.

Their children fled their home villages, went to universities, learned English, travelled, mixed with foreigners. By their nature they were a society that drifted, being young and free from responsibilities, but they drifted slowly. People stayed weeks, months, or just a few days. They went to Athens, they came back from Athens. They sat in cafes and bars drinking coffee and talking for hours, or went to the sea, or to the mountains.

Jayne found it easy to be accepted and easy to get people to talk. Travel experiences and travel plans were obvious topics. The more intellectual among them tackled history and Homer, the pleasure-seekers discussed parties, beaches and sightseeing.

The Delphinians divided public opinion. One view held that they were harmless, a sort of history society crossed with a Greek Woodstock, paying homage to the region's ancient culture while improving tourism. Others rejected the movement as an excuse for young people to behave wildly and for drunk tourists to flood the town.

Jayne decided to seek them out herself. The movement had gained a kind of official status due to the festivals they organised, and had a small office in the town. It was at the back of a bookshop that specialised in Greek history and mythology, at least judging by many of the book covers and posters in the window.

Jayne said that she was interested in the cultural events they organised and would like to join.

"We don't have membership," the woman there told her. "We are a harmony: all are welcome."

She gave Jayne a brochure in English, listing events for the month. There was one that weekend, a moonlight recital of the Odyssey at Delphi followed by wine. It sounded surprisingly sedate without any suggestion of raving Maenads.

Jayne had found out one other fact about Maria Tsakalotos. There was mention of an "English boyfriend" and speculation that she had disappeared with him. He had not been seen since, either.

As with the Delphinians, there were two Marias according to public perception. There was the dutiful young Patras woman who worked for her uncle and had vanished in mysterious and worrying circumstances. Then there was the impulsive, party-loving girl who had ditched her job, left her uncle high and dry and jetted off who-knows-where with her foreign boyfriend. If she was dead, opinion was doing her a huge injustice, Jayne thought.

She was becoming uncomfortable in the town. She knew she had been asking a lot of questions, though they were spread out widely, and no one so far had shown obvious suspicion of her. But there was a limit as to how far she could take it. Much information was volunteered with minimal prompting as gossip was a popular pastime. The mere sight of her Delphinians brochure on a cafe table was enough to spark a lecture on the morals of youth today, or recommendations of historic sites.

A day in Patras, where Maria was from, would be a welcome break. She might even stay overnight. There were regular buses and the route was said to be scenic. Jayne had not managed to fit in a visit there during the holiday with her cousins, so now would be a perfect opportunity.

Yiannis, who had become her unofficial guide, advised on taking a private car. "The bus takes many hours and you may not find it comfortable," he said.

Jayne was quite happy to go at a more leisurely pace. She could always get a car for the return journey if the bus ride there turned out to be too much of an ordeal. The bus was not particularly modern, but there were few passengers that day and travelling along the coast road allowed beautiful views of the sea.

Everything is surrounded by sea here, she thought. It transformed the entire culture. She remembered a schoolteacher mentioning that Greek sailors couldn't swim. It seemed all the more absurd once you saw the place.

Patras lay long and low on the Peloponnese peninsula, backed by the foothills of Mount Panachaikon, hazy green in the shimmering noon heat. The obligatory landmark was the Roman Odeon which Jayne visited and admired, liking the fact that it had been restored for modern use. It contrasted with the long-dead shells of temples and shrines around Delphi.

Several people, including Yiannis and the man at the bus ticket office, had urged her to visit Patras's renowned Turkish baths. But it wasn't Jayne's kind of thing at all. If you went swimming in a public pool that was one thing, but to hang around bathing all day, and worse - to be rubbed and scrubbed by a complete stranger - that was not an experience she would find relaxing.

Instead she went to Patras Castle, from where one could see far across Patras. Watching the view, she listened to the chatter of two nearby American girls taking photographs.

"Georgios says the party's tomorrow night," one said. "We'll have to get the Delphi bus tomorrow."

"Will we get somewhere to stay?" the other asked, a sandy-haired girl.

"No need, it goes on all night. We can hitch to Athens the next morning," her friend said. "Georgios says you can get anything there, it's like candy." They moved off.

They would be on the same bus as Jayne unless she took a cab. It surely couldn't be the same event though?

That evening she wondered if she should try to follow up her only lead, the missing Maria. Her family was from somewhere in Patras. But it just seemed too hard. Jayne had selected a small hotel called the Dionysian, located in the centre of town, rather than one of the more modern blocks lining the seafront. The Dionysian had blue shutters and an orange tree outside and Jayne's room looked out towards the mountain.

At the reception she asked to see a telephone directory. It was in Greek but she was starting to become more familiar with some of the letters, and had written down Maria's name in Greek from the posters in the Spyros taverna. She eventually found Tsakalotos. There weren't endless columns of them but there were enough that it would take a few days to go through them if she struck unlucky and picked the correct one last. Also Patras was a much larger city and getting around on foot would be significantly harder.

She was so tired. She would leave it for now; she could always return another day armed with Maria's father's initials.

Jayne had dropped her plans to get a cab in favour of the bus again. It would make her later back in the town than she had planned, but her curiosity had been piqued by the two American girls.

She waited for them to arrive, and made sure they got on the bus before her. Picking a seat a couple of rows behind her, she put her sunglasses on, leant her head back, and pretended to sleep.

The two girls talked for a while about unrelated things. Boyfriends, the high price of camera films, food they had eaten that they found strange. Jayne had nearly dozed off when finally they mentioned the party again.

"Is it safe, do you think?" The redhead was the more cautious of the pair.

"Georgios says it's fine. They do some poetry or something first, then the police leave them alone. It all starts later."

"I hope there's some good stuff."

"Georgios says they have something special here that's like flying, for hours. He says the oracles used it. You can't get it anywhere else."

So it was the same event that Jayne was planning to attend, organised by the Delphinians. A more eventful night than originally anticipated lay ahead.

9

Back at the Villa Kallina, a surprise awaited her: Lucas. He had managed to fly out a day early.

It felt such a relief to see another English person. She wanted to talk nineteen to the dozen but found herself tongue-tied.

"I haven't yet checked in anywhere, I didn't want to miss you in case you were going out again," he said.

"Surely you can stay here? There are three bedrooms. It seems a waste for it to be just me," Jayne said, then felt a rush of embarrassment. Of course he would have to decline given the circumstances. She silently berated herself for having put him on the spot.

But there was no awkwardness. "I would be delighted."

Jayne helped Lucas to one of the unused rooms and left him to unpack. She went to the kitchen to fetch him a glass of water. She hadn't used the kitchen at all except for getting drinks; the food at the various tavernas was so cheap, and there was no cooking or clearing up for her to worry about.

"You've been away?" Lucas noted her small suitcase.

"I stayed in Patras overnight, on a bit of a whim. If nothing else it delivered me something of a warning regarding my plans this evening." She explained about the poetry recital and the secret festivities afterwards.

"That sounds like a wonderful night. I hope you don't mind if I accompany you?" Lucas said.

Jayne felt a sudden joy. Then concern as she realised that her feelings were not as neutral towards Lucas as they should have been. She consoled herself that perhaps it was just a reaction from finally seeing a familiar face.

"Of course, I would be delighted."

The poetry recital wasn't for a few more hours so they went for an early dinner in the town. Jayne chose the harbourside taverna from where she had seen Caroline. In her head she thought of it as the "Caroline Taverna", just as the Apollo was the "Yiannis taverna". The Greek names merged into one another here, and it was easier to pin her thoughts on people.

She wanted Lucas to realise the distance she had seen Caroline at, from the actual table. She encouraged him to take the seat she had previously used - since they were early, there was a choice of tables - and pointed out the distances to him.

Conveniently a couple of people walked past at just that moment.

"I do see what you mean. There really is little doubt that you could mistake a face from just these couple of yards," Lucas said.

Jayne hadn't really needed to feel vindicated since Lucas already believed her, but it felt like she had checked off another detail.

Despite Jayne's inner turmoil Lucas was a wonderful companion. He set her at ease and always managed to give the impression that he enjoyed other people's company. She had seen this with Harry during the lunch in London, even though that meal had ended on a sourer note. Jayne didn't dare flatter herself that Lucas enjoyed being with her that much, the circumstances were too sad and surely he would rather be spending time with his fiancée.

"I should tell you what I have been up to," he said. "You probably thought I was being idle, but the truth is I didn't like to say too much over the phone. I had to look up a couple of friends in rather privileged positions, and if anything attracts a tap on the line, it's that. As much to monitor them as me, doubtless, but why take the risk?"

Having assumed phone tapping to be the domain of the KGB, Jayne was alarmed to imagine Scotland Yard listening into her line.

Lucas continued. "I have an old schoolfriend who now works in an intelligence-related position. Of course he couldn't directly tell me whether any of our suspicions are sound, or whether we're barking up the wrong tree. But he was able to not-tell me in a very helpful way.

"Importantly, I asked him straight out if it was an accident or a deliberate killing. He couldn't tell me as such, but again from his non-tell it was apparent that they all think it's the latter."

"Lucas, I'm so sorry," Jayne said.

"We wanted answers, didn't we? And perhaps it's kinder to Caroline's memory to consider that she didn't die by folly or even bad luck. Someone chose to end her life. We just need some proof of whom and how and why."

Lucas's choice of words was interesting. He sought proof, not facts. Did he already have a theory, and just need evidence to corroborate it? Not for the first time Jayne wondered if Lucas knew or at least suspected who might be responsible for Caroline's death. She had enough questions in her own mind. Perhaps she should be grateful if his reticence spared her a few more.

"Another visit I made was to an old acquaintance who previously worked in intelligence. He was more free to speak, and was useful for getting possibilities of the kinds of groups Caroline might have been monitoring," Lucas said.

"Unfortunately there are so many that it rather widens the trail than narrows it. There are dissident elements still sore over the Civil War, years ago though it was. There are Soviet-backed communist factions fomenting trouble. Bulgarians, Albanians and Yugoslavians are all meddling. As is Russia itself, both through direct and indirect means. There are drugs, a great of drugs, partly because Greece is a conduit from East to West. Some of the trafficking is solely a business in itself, but some is thought to be funding certain groups. There's a huge amount of smuggling - no surprise perhaps, on any trade route - guns, gold, antiquities."

Jayne felt overwhelmed.

"It hinders rather than it helps, doesn't it?" Lucas said. "Still, it may explain the vanishing of the other girl, if she was mixed up in that Delphi group. Easy to stumble across something she shouldn't have, the wrong people talking at the wrong time."

"I had rather ruled her out," Jayne said. "It seems she had an English boyfriend and no one has seen him since either, so perhaps they just went off travelling together. Though if you're a nice dutiful Greek girl, as many seem to think she was, you would surely at least write a note for your family or make a telephone call. There's no suggestion of any row either. I did dig around a bit."

Lucas divided the rest of the wine between them.

"The final thing, from my second acquaintance, is that he considers the circumstances of Caroline's death bizarre if the motive is political. Had it been carried out by one of the factions it would have been swift and carefully planned; most likely she would just have disappeared. Dumping a body in water is messy and unpredictable. It's an amateur method, and these people are anything but amateurs."

"So it would make more sense if it wasn't Caroline and was instead this other girl, perhaps killed by her boyfriend, the mysterious Englishman. Maybe they had a row and he killed her in a fit of passion, without planning. The sea would seem a perfect place to drop a body, particularly if you had no idea of the tides."

"Possibly. But I don't really believe in *crimes de passion*. Murder is usually much more mundane, generally about money."

"That's exactly what John Lambert, our barrister friend, claims," Jayne said. "One question I do have: how do the police identify a body, particularly in these kind of circumstances?"

"That's another odd point. Identification was obviously made quite rapidly, given the speed with which they notified her family. There are so many young women here. If she was diving, she wouldn't have had identity papers directly on her."

"That's what I wondered. But if on the other hand someone was deliberately trying to fake the identity, might they make it deliberately easy? Perhaps leave a bag with a passport in it by the shore, or something? Or they could report Caroline missing, then wait for the other girl's body to be found, then identify her as Caroline. Except you said that Harry made the formal identification," Jayne said.

"Formal yes, because he is family, but it's possible someone else misidentified her first. If so there should of course be a record."

Jayne frowned. "That's where I went wrong with the police. I was more concerned with finding out where she had been staying, and where exactly they found her. I didn't even think to ask for those details. What a waste! We'll have to go back."

"We'll see in the morning. For now, the Oracle awaits us."

10

The first row at the theatre at Delphi was already taken up with people so Lucas and Jayne sat in the second row, which was about half full. The ancient theatre originally accommodated five thousand people according to Jayne's guidebook but much of the uppermost seating area was now crumbling.

While it wasn't quite a toga party, some effort had been made by many audience members to dress with respect to ancient Greek costume and a lot of people were wearing white. Jayne was rather glad to have chosen a white sundress as she blended more with the crowd. The night air was cool on her skin and she wrapped a stole around her.

On came the performers who had clearly taken pains with their costumes. Jayne felt that a somewhat stout, bearded man would have done better to wear the looser draped robes of his colleagues than his disconcertingly short garment, banded with leather across the chest.

Lucas suppressed a smile. "Even though we won't understand a word, at least they're giving us a spectacle," he said.

There followed one of the dullest hours Jayne had ever had the misfortune to sit through. Cade's Bosnian drama was a treat by comparison. Bearded men and a very earnest woman declaimed verse after verse in Ancient Greek with no break or explanatory notes, despite the flyer advertising the event having been written in both Greek and English.

Jayne was also on edge about what might be happening later. The current crowd certainly didn't look like a wild set of partygoers. To sit for an hour enraptured by Homer and then dance and carouse until dawn just didn't seem likely.

Finally the performance and some sort of encore was complete, to polite applause. Glasses and carafes of retsina suddenly appeared and a staid sort of drinks party formed. It must have been around nine o'clock now; the evening was darkening rapidly. Candles were lit around the stage. Someone gently plucked the strings of a lyre. It was all deceptively pleasant.

But Jayne noticed people slipping into the shadows, drifting up the hillside rather than back down to where the road and cars and taxis were. She nudged Lucas. "Should we follow them?"

He took her arm and when a couple near them turned to leave, he and Jayne walked along too. Further up they saw people inside one of the wayside shrines, holding flashlights. They had moved a slab of stone from the floor, and were hauling up crates of wine from a cellar below.

Edward Turbeville

"It looks like they're well stocked," Lucas said. "A useful place to keep the drink cool and out of sight during the day."

The route eventually took them to the stadium. At the far end they saw the glow of torches and a large throng of people. At one side was a band of musicians preparing to play. "Where did all these people come from?" Jayne asked. "There are definitely more here than at the recital. They must have just come straight up while we were all sitting there listening."

"Lucky them," Lucas said.

She was looking out for the two American girls but hadn't yet managed to see if they were there. They might be hard to spot amid the crowd, which was still growing, and the limited light. Plus there were so many young women here of a similar age.

The band started playing a strange melange of Greek folk music and more modern melodies. It was very rhythmic, almost feverish, with no singer, just a violin that sounded more and more frenzied as its music flowed forth. Jayne had preferred the more sedate music of the lyre earlier and she wasn't much of a dancer, particularly at this pace. But the crowd enveloped them and she was pressed towards Lucas. He smiled at her, putting his arms around her like the other couples dancing, and they moved to the rhythm. There were many people dancing solo as well, arms waving in the air, some clearly intoxicated already. By drugs or drink, Jayne couldn't tell.

She was both uncomfortable and thrilled by being so close to Lucas. She didn't attribute any other motive to their dancing than the need to mix in with the other revellers, but she still hadn't felt this way since Rory

60

danced with her once at a May ball. Cade's right, I have been cloistered, Jayne thought. She must be careful not to make a fool of herself.

They were interrupted by a tap on the shoulder from a short Greek youth with very dark, beetling brows that nearly met in the middle and a somewhat simian grin. He drew a small pouch from the inner lining of his jacket and raised his eyebrows questioningly, his smile fixed.

Lucas squeezed Jayne's shoulder twice, firmly. It wasn't any pre-agreed signal but Jayne took it to mean something like "go along with this". They went with the man to the edge of the area, pushing their way through the dancers, to where people were sitting around on the large stone blocks.

The monkey-man opened his pouch and showed the contents to Lucas. Jayne hadn't a clue what they were, drugs obviously, but she had no idea what kind.

The man and Lucas were negotiating, with Lucas holding up five fingers. Eventually a transaction took place and the vendor slipped away, presumably to do more business.

Jayne asked Lucas what he had bought.

"Some cannabis resin by the look of it, though for all the faith I have in that fellow it may be boot polish and oregano," he said. "A drink would be better." They had seen people holding glasses on the other side of the dancing area. Jayne longed for something other than cheap retsina but didn't hold out much hope.

Lucas led her back through the dancing. The music took a sudden change of tempo, appearing to double its pace, and the crowd surged, breaking them apart. People had formed into a chain which crossed between Jayne and

Lucas. Before she could try and find her way around it, hands grabbed her waist from behind, and seconds later she was thrust towards someone else's back.

More to steady herself she clasped the person in front's waist and became part of the line of revellers. It wound around, she was twisted and jerked right and left, and just as she thought she would pass near Lucas again, the person behind her broke contact.

Suddenly someone else grabbed her, and before she could cry out, a hand clapped over her mouth, and she was wrenched across to the other side of the area. There was a rag against her face, a sweet, acetone like smell. Then darkness.

Jayne came round, finding her arms tied to her sides, not very tightly but enough to constrain her from easy or rapid movement. Her head was full of fog and she felt a little bruised.

There were stone blocks around her but she could see the night sky above and ahead. She could still hear music faintly. She must still be at Delphi. In one of the ruined shrines? How much time had elapsed?

"Don't move!" a voice hissed at her. It was a voice she recognised.

Someone came forward holding a torch. It was Yiannis.

"You shouldn't be here," he said. "You asked too many questions."

"How long have I been here?"

"Not long. Less than half an hour," he told her.

"What are you going to do?"

"I'm here to warn you. Go home. Go back to England. It's not safe for you here."

Jayne was in a state of shock, she was terrified, and her head ached and felt foggy. Despite this she sensed that Yiannis was also nervous.

"Where's Lucas?" she asked. "He'll be looking for me."

"They won't deal with him as nicely as with you," Yiannis warned. "You need to go."

"Who's they?"

Her behaviour was rattling him. He had expected tears, pleas, compliance.

"You don't have to know that. They will hurt you. I'm acting as your friend," he said. To some extent Jayne believed him. She certainly wasn't scared of him but his paymasters were a different story.

"Did they hurt Caroline? Or Maria? Is this about drugs?" Jayne asked.

"No questions!" Yiannis said. "If I untie you, you have to go home and then you have to leave. Tomorrow. You can't stay here. You're lucky I gave you this chance."

"How can I leave now, Yiannis, now I know there is someone out there?"

"You can't bring the dead back," Yiannis said. "Just leave it alone."

"So they're dead? Both of them?"

He was getting exasperated with her. "Time is running out. You need to be gone from here."

"I can't leave without Lucas. He'll go straight to the police," Jayne said.

"You think they'll help you?"

"I think for enough drachma they'll do anything," Jayne said. "The question is how much more your people are prepared to pay."

"They're not my people."

"So why are you doing this?" Jayne asked. "What's in it for you? Money I suppose."

Yiannis looked slightly ashamed. Jayne thought how she had always liked him since their short acquaintance. Despite this bizarre abduction, she thought that he was fundamentally a decent man. The pay had just been too generous on this occasion. Or perhaps they had found other means to coerce him?

"Can you get away from this?" she asked him. "Or are you in too deep?"

"I don't know what you mean."

"If you stop dealing with them, would you be safe? Would you be safe in Athens?"

She was turning the tables, casting him as the victim.

"They are in Athens too."

"London then."

For a second his eyes lit up. "But how would I get to London?"

"We'll help you. Find you a job even. But first you have to help me. If you can get me the information I need, I will go. Lucas too."

Yiannis was considering it. "You can't come to the bar any more. I'll find somewhere else. But please make your bookings. They need to know that you are leaving. It's not safe for anyone if you stay here."

"Once I have what I want, I'll leave," Jayne said. "I'm not interested in trying to bring down this organisation, the Delphinians, if they are the ones that put you up to this. We merely want to know what happened to Caroline. Meanwhile you can tell them that you've successfully intimidated me and I'm rushing back to England as quick as I can."

"OK," Yiannis said, very reluctantly. "But you have to go back to your villa. This party isn't for you."

Lucas was horrified to learn of what had happened when Jayne finally found him. He had been searching for her for nearly an hour. He wanted to call the police and insisted that she be taken to hospital. But Jayne assured him she was alright.

"There's no point going to the police. I'm fine. I haven't even been robbed, and it would just stir up more trouble," she said.

"You should see a doctor at least. You were unconscious."

Jayne promised him that if she felt ill in the night or the next morning, she would do so. "For now I feel fine. I don't appear to have bumped my head or anything. Besides which, I think it would be difficult finding a doctor at this hour."

"You may be right. Still, I feel very uncomfortable about this. It's my fault that you're even here at all."

"If I was worried about the risk I wouldn't have come. I had a point to prove as well, remember."

"Well, at least I'll be nearby tonight. If you feel unwell at all, you must call me," he said.

They were walking back down the hillside towards the road. Lucas had given her his arm, and she used it to steady herself a couple of times.

"This could actually be a good thing," Jayne said. "Now we'll get the information we need, and more quickly."

Lucas studied her closely. "Christ, you're stoic," he said. "Most people - men or women - would be packing their suitcases in fright."

"I think from the start it just seemed so very amateur. Poor Yiannis. I wasn't even tied very well," Jayne said. "If he'd left me, I could easily have run off, at least once my legs were a bit firmer. And now he's almost on our side."

She stumbled slightly on a stony part of the path, but corrected herself.

"There is one other thing. One, maybe twice, I'm sure Yiannis started to say "he" and then switched to "they". I may have imagined it. But somehow, I got the sense that there was an individual behind this."

"That is information I will certainly extract from him," Lucas said.

They had reached the road now, where despite the late hour there were a couple of taxis waiting at the site.

"They obviously know about the party," Jayne said. They took one of the cabs, and rode back to the villa. Jayne suddenly realised it would be Lucas's first night under the same roof as her. She found that this made her many magnitudes more nervous than she had been when tied up in the temple with Yiannis trying to threaten her. Poor Yiannis, she thought again. It would almost be amusing if it weren't for the deaths, now confirmed, and her concerns for his safety.

11

They had breakfast together in the Villa Kallina. Lucas had gone out early for provisions. It was the first time Jayne had used the kitchen, given her constant frequenting of the bars and tavernas.

The previous night had not been awkward. Jayne had suddenly been hit by such a wave of tiredness - delayed shock, Lucas told her - that she had nearly fallen asleep in the taxi. She went to bed as soon as they arrived and slept through to morning.

In the small courtyard behind the villa they ate bread and honey, olives, and strong black coffee that Lucas brewed. It was an unusual breakfast but Jayne was ravenous. The morning sun was warm already, despite the early hour.

"I'm not sure if we should wait here to see if Yiannis has decided to help out, or just go to the police station and try a few drachma there," she said.

"We can give it some more time here. There's no rush."

Edward Turbeville

Sure enough, not long after they had cleared the breakfast things away there was a face at the kitchen window. It was Yiannis. He hissed at Jayne.

"Meet me in one hour in Pythas square. It's the one with the two orange trees, past the Ecclesia Maria."

One hour passed and they made their way to the little square. It didn't seem the wisest choice of location, being surrounded by buildings. Jayne wondered for a moment if it might be a trap. She mentioned this to Lucas.

"Rather foolish to try anything in broad daylight, I should think."

They waited in the shade of a tree. Eventually Yiannis arrived, alone, looking suitably furtive.

"Come," he said, and headed into an alleyway. Cautiously they followed him.

The alley took a couple of turns, at one point opening out into another small courtyard before narrowing between two buildings again. Finally Yiannis reached a blue door, and ushered them inside. They were surprised to find themselves in a small bar with just a few tables, and two very ancient Greek men playing a form of backgammon.

"It is for locals only," Yiannis told them. "No police, no interference."

"No Delphinians?" Lucas said.

Yiannis grimaced. "I am not one of them."

"Why don't you explain from the beginning?"

Yiannis's story of the Delphinians was pretty much what they had already worked out. It was ostensibly a historical society, dedicated to promoting Ancient Greek culture. It had been successful in attracting the support and participation of many earnest people, even scholars associated with leading universities. Through these connections the society arranged educational visas for assorted agitators from Eastern bloc countries. Drug money kept things comfortably afloat. Backpackers, travellers and students from nearby universities were a lucrative, conveniently itinerant market. None of them stayed around long enough to notice anything beyond the educational events and parties.

Yiannis wasn't sure what the Delphinians' long term aims were, but he had heard rumours of weapons smuggling and even assassination mentioned. Whoever was behind it clearly had political aims. This made sense, given the involvement of MI6.

"What about Maria Tsakalotos, what was her involvement?"

Maria, according to Yiannis, had joined just for the parties. "She wasn't involved with anything, so far as I know. But I think she found something out perhaps. People talk, they are overheard. Then what do you do? I keep my mouth shut. But even that wasn't good enough this time," he said. It had become known that Jayne was asking questions. There was concern. Yiannis had been tasked with scaring her off.

"They paid me money, but it wasn't about the money," he said. "If I refused, they could make things very difficult for me here. You would be ok, you could go overseas. You weren't important enough to kill. But you might have become so, if you stumbled across something like Maria did. I was doing you a favour," he said in justification.

"You might have just spoken with me. Chloroform and a rope were rather unnecessary."

Yiannis looked embarrassed. "I saw too many films I think. I should have worn a mask."

"I would have recognised your voice."

"And Maria's English boyfriend? Was he involved?" Lucas asked.

Yiannis looked surprised. "She didn't have a boyfriend that I knew of. There was an Englishman, a tall man, around sometimes. I think he was an actual historian though. You know how it is here, so many people."

"What about Caroline?" Jayne asked. "Why was Maria's body identified as Caroline's?"

Yiannis shrugged. "Someone got her papers, swapped them for Maria's. Maybe they never meant her to die. Maybe they confused Maria and Caroline." It was clear he didn't know.

Jayne looked at the two elderly Greek men playing their board game. If you had to describe them superficially, it would be a nearly identical description. Of course they might be brothers. But the basic physical details were the same. "Eighty something, short to medium height, white hair, clean shaven." How much more could one say? Just as with Caroline and Maria: female, twenties, slim, medium height, long dark hair.

"But you said they were both dead?" Jayne said.

"I didn't say because I don't know. But if she was a spy, it's likely."

It was disconcerting to hear Caroline described as a spy, but Jayne supposed that she effectively had such. How strange to think of Caroline, so studious, so conventional, carrying out this kind of work. Risking her life and apparently forfeiting it.

"Can you tell us who these people are, the ones who communicated with you?" Lucas asked.

"I don't know their names. I might recognise them, but I hadn't seen them before, and also not since," Yiannis said.

"Anyway you needn't worry about me anymore," Jayne said. "We're both going to leave this afternoon, for Athens, if that's quick enough for you?"

"It's wise," he said.

Lucas gave Yiannis his address in London. "As promised," he said, "if you make it over we'll do our best to help you."

The plan was to head to Athens, to the airport, but then to slip away and visit Patras. There they would hire a car and try to track down the right Tsakalotos household. For some reason it was the Englishman that most interested Jayne. Even if he wasn't involved, why had he just disappeared?

First Lucas would pay a visit to the local police, for a final attempt at obtaining information. Jayne would remain behind at the villa, with Lucas insisting that the doors were locked.

While Lucas was gone she phoned Cade. He didn't even give her time to update him before breaking in and speaking urgently.

"I've been waiting for your call, I had no idea how to contact you," he said. "I have something to tell you, that I should have told you before. No, not over the phone. You'll understand why when you know what it is."

"I'll be back the day after tomorrow. We're just going back to Patras first."

"It can't wait that long. Can you get back sooner? Today even? I'll meet you at the airport."

"Cade what on earth is wrong?" Jayne said, disconcerted. "Are you in trouble?"

"No, but you have to know this before you go on with your mission, or quest, whatever it is."

"And you absolutely can't tell me or even give a hint over the telephone?"

"It's too complicated," Cade said.

"I'll do what I can," Jayne promised. "I'll call you from Athens before I board. If I can get a flight by this afternoon. It might be a rather late night arrival."

Lucas returned from the police station with scant new information. No amount of drachmas had prised any further documents out of them. "I don't have your persuasive touch," he said to Jayne.

Jayne told him about Cade's call.

"He gave no idea what it was, nothing at all?"

"None, except that it was contingent on our investigation," Jayne said.

They decided to travel together to Athens as planned. There Jayne would try to get on a plane, and if there were no seats that evening, she would take the dawn flight. It reached London by early morning thanks to the time difference.

Jayne was sorry to be leaving. Although it wasn't a holiday it had been an exhilarating experience and she greatly enjoyed Lucas's company. She looked at the boats, the blue sky, the birds swooping over the water. It was a paradise in its own way. It should be enough, but it wasn't. People always wanted more.

Death at Delphi

PART TWO

LIGHT THICKENS

12

A very sombre Aubrey met her at the airport. "Thank god I spoke with Francis earlier today and he mentioned you were coming," he said. "I'm afraid he's been in an accident."

Jayne went pale. "What's happened? You don't mean he's dead?"

"No, but not far from it I regret to say. It was a car accident, a hit and run as he was on his way to the theatre. He's in St Mary's hospital, at Paddington.

"Can we visit him?"

"I'm taking you straight there. You should eat first, but I know you won't. Much good will it do, since he's unconscious. They don't even know if..." he broke off. "Anyway, that's for the doctors."

Outside it was raining, and Aubrey opened an enormous black umbrella which he held over her while they went to find a taxi. What a dear friend he was, thought Jayne, amid her shock.

Arriving at the hospital and entering through the usual corridors and lifts and doors to intensive care was a blur. Cade lay there, in a room by himself, his eyes closed, hooked up to various machines.

"His beautiful face is spared," Aubrey said.

"How did it happen exactly? Where is he injured?"

"So far as I understand it, he had some luck. He was struck in the shoulder but it was more of a glancing impact. That flung him over in some manner, and he rolled - mitigating the force of it - but hitting his head as he fell. They're monitoring his brain. Amazingly nothing is broken, limbs and things anyway."

Jayne saw that part of Cade's hair was shaved, with wires taped to it. She looked at the notes on the clipboard at the foot of the bed. "Francis Cade". He hadn't changed it formally then, even though only his family and Aubrey still used his first name. "How did they manage to notify you?"

"I'm down as next of kin, with his mother so far away." Oh god, Cade's mother. She was a widow who lived in the North East.

Jayne looked questioningly at Aubrey. "Have you managed to contact her?"

"Yes, as soon as I heard. Mrs Cade is on her way. I've got a key to Francis's place if you'd like to stay there, or you're very welcome to stay with me. Both you and his mother, there's plenty of room. Or I'll arrange a hotel. Whatever you're most comfortable with."

"I think I'd like to stay with you, if you have room."

"It's a mansion of a flat," Aubrey assured her. His family was extremely wealthy and a great-uncle had left him a property in Bloomsbury. "Now we should eat, because we'll need to keep our strength up."

"I can't bear to leave him alone," Jayne said.

"He'll be out for hours, they've put him in an induced coma," Aubrey said. He looked at his watch. "Mrs Cade should be at King's Cross in an hour. Her name is Margaret, I believe."

He took her to one of his clubs, a gloomy place with elderly gentleman sunk deep into leather armchairs of similarly ancient vintage.

"Now it's about time someone explained to me what is going on," Aubrey said, when they were about half way through the meal.

"It's all such a complicated mess. It started with Caroline, and when I thought I saw her in Greece." Jayne gave Aubrey a basic outline of events.

"And you were rushing back at Francis's request?" Aubrey asked.

"Yes. I don't suppose you have any knowledge of what it was? Even a faint idea?"

"I'm afraid not," Aubrey said. "These past few days I've been on the South Coast, attending estate sales. I did hear one piece of news. It appears that the engagement between John and Lucy is no more. Amanda mentioned it when I rang her about the accident."

Poor Mrs Cade was in a terrible state when they met her. Her son at death's door, a four hour train journey, and Jayne suspected the expenses of London were an added pressure. Cade's family had very little money.

"Aubrey's asked us both to stay with him," Jayne told her as they arrived at the hospital. "I hope that will suit you?" Now Mrs Cade didn't have to worry about hotels at least, or be surrounded by all of Cade's things in his tiny Hammersmith flat.

It was nearly midnight and apart from the nurse on duty as they entered the floor, there wasn't anyone else about. Patients were sleeping or unconscious. Machines beeped and hummed softly through the hush.

They reached Cade's room, and Jayne ushered his mother inside and encouraged her to sit down by the bed, as she looked near collapse.

"Francis is stable, the doctors say, and that's a good thing," Jayne said. "I'll go and see if I can find a doctor to speak with you." She thought that Mrs Cade might like some private time with her son.

Aubrey was one step ahead of her and had already tracked down a young Asian doctor. He looked like he hadn't slept in several days, which he probably hadn't, being a junior doctor, Jayne thought.

The doctor was able to spend a few minutes with Mrs Cade. His position gave him more authority in persuading her to go home for the night than either Jayne or Aubrey could have done. He reassured them that Cade wouldn't wake before the morning and would be carefully monitored all night.

Back at Aubrey's flat in Bloomsbury - though flat seemed inadequate to describe such a palatial suite of rooms - Jayne busied herself with helping Mrs Cade off to bed and fetching towels for her. Aubrey offered her a hot drink but she would only take a glass of water.

Jayne also declined a cup of tea. "We all need a good night's sleep. The chances are we'll wake in the early hours from worry anyway," she said. But she was so exhausted she slept through, and didn't wake until the morning sun was streaming through a gap in the curtains, far later than she had intended. She quickly washed and dressed, and joined Aubrey and Mrs Cade for breakfast.

"The doctors do their rounds in the morning, the nurse told me," Aubrey was saying, "and she said visiting hours for intensive care aren't until half past ten. They are quite strict about it." He was more plainly dressed than usual, a white cotton handkerchief replacing the usual colourful silk squares in his top pocket.

Jayne didn't like to say "good morning" since it clearly wasn't, so she asked Mrs Cade if she had been comfortable and managed to sleep at all. Aubrey left them alone to go and make some coffee.

"We can visit Francis's flat if you like, Mrs Cade, when visiting hours close. We'll get him some clean clothes for when he leaves hospital." Jayne was well aware that it would be some time before Cade was released, days or even weeks, but she correctly guessed that his mother would want to keep busy.

"Call me Margaret, please dear. You've both been so kind. I worry so much about Francis being down here. But this is the kind of thing that could happen anywhere, isn't it? It's not like a mugging, which is what you expect in London."

For the first time Jayne found herself wondering how the accident had happened, and what the police were doing about it. There was a tiny, nagging fear in her head that she was trying to suppress. Hit and runs happened every day, in every city: a careless driver, panicking, fleeing the scene. There was absolutely no reason to consider it might be anything else.

"Won't you have some more tea?" Margaret Cade wasn't a coffee drinker, and Jayne sensed that she had been rather alarmed by some of Aubrey's more exotic breakfast items. Fortunately there had been plenty of toast and marmalade.

The next morning the doctors were pleased with Cade's condition. There was no swelling on his brain, his heartbeat was strong, and he had a little more colour than the pallor of the previous day. While Margaret sat with him, holding his hand and talking to him (though they had warned her that he wouldn't wake yet), Jayne spoke to Aubrey outside. It was the first chance they had had to speak alone that day.

"Aubrey, was there anything unusual about the accident? Did the police mention anything?"

"You mean did someone deliberately run him down?" Jayne appreciated how Aubrey got straight to the point.

"Yes. It's just that it must have happened in broad daylight, and that street is quite quiet. I suppose someone may have decided to take it as a short cut, sped up perhaps."

"I've wondered that myself. Nothing was said. I hope the police won't be too crass when it comes to questioning Mrs Cade."

"When will they come, do you think?" Jayne asked.

"When he comes round. Hopefully the doctors can hold them off as long as possible. I doubt he'll remember a thing. Though there's no apparent damage, to his brain I mean, so he may have some memory of it."

"I've suggested to Mrs Cade that she and I go round to Cade's flat later. You have a key, don't you? We can give it a spring clean or something, and keep ourselves occupied."

"Good luck with that," said Aubrey. Cade's place deviated far from his own ideas of domestic order.

Cade's flat was indeed something of mess. It was mainly untidy - at least there weren't piles of food-encrusted dishes or anything. He was clearly less house proud than Aubrey, but who wouldn't be house proud living off Bloomsbury square in a mansion flat furnished with antiques? Besides which Aubrey had a housekeeper who came in daily.

"Oh dear!" Margaret exclaimed, embarrassed on Cade's behalf. "I hoped I'd raised him to keep himself in a better state than this."

"Don't worry. He works such late hours, it can be hard to keep on top of things." Jayne stacked newspapers into a neat pile while Cade's mother saw to his clothes. Suddenly the older woman sat down on the sofa and started to weep.

"Here I am, getting cross about his socks, and there's my boy, my only boy, lying there and not even opening his eyes."

Jayne wished Aubrey's large white handkerchief was to hand. She rummaged under some more papers and unearthed a box of tissues. Mrs Cade dabbed her nose.

"All I've ever wanted for him was to find a nice girl and settle down, start a family. I know he's very talented at his theatre. But they're not good hours for a married life. And now he may never have the chance."

Jayne felt a deep pang of compassion for the woman. Even if Cade recovered - and of course he would, she told herself firmly - there would hardly be a wife and children in the conventional way. Cade was an only child, his mother's hope of grandchildren rested with him alone. Aubrey by contrast had numerous half-siblings, both older and younger, as his parents had married and remarried multiple times. There were already several grandchildren around.

Cade is going to have to tell her one day, Jayne thought, and though she will love him still and accept him, it will kill her hopes and dreams.

"I think we've got on top of things," she said a little later, as Mrs Cade finished some dusting. "Why don't we go and get a quick sandwich, and pick up some flowers and magazines for him?"

Neither of them knew that the magazines would be long out of date before Cade got a chance to read them.

13

Mrs Cade went off to the hospital by herself that afternoon, and Jayne returned to Cade's flat. She was exhausted and thought she might take a nap. She didn't want to over impose on Aubrey, and besides, she was nearer Cade's place.

As she arrived at the building she was surprised to see Caroline's brother Harry just outside. She had hardly given Caroline a thought during the past 24 hours, which the sight of Harry made her feel remiss for.

Harry seemed rather disconcerted.

"Were you expecting to see Cade?" she asked. "I'm afraid he's in hospital, there's been a dreadful accident."

"What happened?" he asked.

"A hit and run it seems. He took a nasty blow and hit his head. But he's alright, he's still unconscious, but they're looking after him well."

"Oh. Thank god."

"Why don't you come inside and we can have some tea. I've got a key," Jayne said.

They sat in Cade's living room, newly spick and span from her and Margaret's efforts. Harry was obviously uneasy.

"I hear you've just been back to Greece," he said.

Jayne suddenly felt some embarrassment. Given Harry was Caroline's brother, but Lucas just a cousin, they should perhaps have kept him more in the loop about their plans.

"Yes, it was Lucas's suggestion. He was concerned that there might be some irregularities," she improvised, "and asked me to help check things out as I was already familiar with the location."

Harry pushed a hand through his hair. He had rather floppy hair, that might have benefitted from a closer cut.

"I know you think you saw her," he said.

"Harry, I..."

He interrupted her. "Hear me out. I think I'm going to have to tell you some things, that I was hoping to keep private."

As he spoke he was fiddling with the fabric on his sleeve, nervously, and looked unhappy.

"The fact is that Caroline didn't die on the first of the month, so you may well have seen her when you thought you did."

After all this time. Jayne felt the last traces of self-doubt lift, and then apprehension.

"The thing is," Harry continued, "and I really wanted to keep this from the family, so I would ask you for your discretion, but Caroline made a suicide attempt and ended up in hospital. That's why the police contacted me and I had to fly over."

Jayne was horrified. She was sure that Caroline was the last person in the world who would have done such a thing, at least according to her memory of her old university friend.

"Are you absolutely certain? Caroline actually tried to kill herself?"

"Yes," Harry said. He looked very uncomfortable. "It was to do with her love life, she wasn't happy."

He was silent for another while, and then spoke up angrily. "This is all Lucas's fault!"

Jayne was taken aback.

"How on earth do you mean?" she asked. "I understood that Lucas cared very dearly for Caroline."

"That's just it, he led her on," Harry said. "He cared for her, but not in that way. It was destroying Caroline. She couldn't take it anymore. She was in Greece, and she got hold of some pills one night, and there you have it."

"I suppose Victoria's presence can't have helped. That must have been hard for her to take."

"Victoria?" Harry looked surprised. "What on earth has Victoria got to do with this?"

"Well, the engagement, obviously. It must have caused Caroline some pain."

"The engagement? Oh yes, I suppose it may have," he said.

"Anyway," Harry continued. "Let me try and relate exactly what happened. I had a phone call from the police that Caroline had overdosed. I flew out there, and then after I arrived, unbeknownst to me, there was some disastrous mix up. A second girl had been admitted to the hospital on the same day, of similar age, after a diving accident, but they couldn't save her. Caroline was fine, but there was a confusion, and they took me to the wrong person, in the morgue.

"You can imagine the shock. I have to confess I couldn't quite bring myself to look. She was covered, but I could see her hair. I felt I didn't need to get a closer look. I feel beyond awful about that now.

"Meanwhile before there was even a chance to set things straight, Caroline discharged herself, without even knowing I was there. The nurses didn't tell her, because they didn't know I was there either, since I had been sent to the morgue earlier rather than the ward. I didn't find out about the mix-up for several days, long after I had already returned. But of course by then it was too late, because they were calling me to tell me that she had obtained more pills and killed herself. The horror I felt from that second notification, it was a thousand times worse."

He buried his face in his hands.

"Because of me, she's dead," he said. "If only I had managed to find her, during that week, but there was no one there for her."

Jayne was horrified by everything Harry had said. It was very hard to take in.

"What about the burial?" she asked.

"The correct body was repatriated, I managed to sort that out at least," Harry said. "I feel like I was given a second chance, and blew it. No one can ever know - it would cause the family too much more pain. Better that they think it was an accident than that she took her own life."

He was trying to persuade her now to keep his secret.

"I didn't want to tell you. But you might have found something out, and it could have caused a terrible drama. My parents are already suffering so much."

What a tragic mess. And all because Harry had been too afraid to make a proper identification. Jayne checked herself. She was being unfair. The original mix up wasn't his fault, and he would have been very shocked and upset. Ultimately if it had been Caroline's choice to commit suicide, Harry couldn't be held to blame. It was just very sad and frustrating how nearly the situation could have been resolved. Or might have, she supposed, as there was no guarantee that Harry would have been able to change Caroline's intentions.

Still, Jayne couldn't reconcile this image of Caroline - despairing, alone, suicidal - with her own memory of her. But then hadn't she also been just as surprised at Caroline's secret career?

"I am very sorry to hear all this Harry," Jayne said. "And I appreciate you confiding in me. I certainly didn't intend to cause any further distress, and nor did Lucas, by our queries. I had of course wondered about a mix-up, because of my sighting of her, and the dates making no sense. But my hope was that we might find her alive. And I will certainly keep your secret. I see no reason to cause your parents any more pain."

"Thank you," Harry said. He paused for a moment. "I would also rather you didn't tell Lucas. Out of respect for Caroline. I don't think he really deserves to know how he destroyed her happiness."

He really hates Lucas, Jayne thought. But perhaps it was understandable given the circumstances.

"Of course." She would have to find some other reason to explain her withdrawal from their inquiries. Then she remembered something else.

"Just one more thing, Harry. When I saw Caroline, she seemed to be at work, or on some kind of professional outing. It just seems strange, given the circumstances, that she would have gone back, only to kill herself, what, a day or two days later?"

"Two days I believe," Harry said. "Who knows what may have happened in that time, what torment she went through psychologically?"

He looked at her, as if hesitating for a moment. "Also, and perhaps you may know this, but Caroline was involved in some government work, so to speak."

"Yes, I had heard something along those lines."

"She may have thought that it would be jeopardising the situation if she deserted her duty. I like to think that she considered such things, despite everything, until the end."

14

Harry had given Jayne a lot to think about. Or perhaps it was the opposite: had his revelations really closed the book? Now Caroline's sad tale was told, perhaps it was time to move on.

More days passed and Cade had still not regained consciousness, to the increasing concern of his doctors. They couldn't determine why so there was nothing to do except wait. Jayne, feeling slightly ashamed, used Cade's condition as an excuse to avoid Lucas. She didn't feel that she could face him yet, given what she knew.

Even though it wasn't really Lucas's fault, and Harry - out of brotherly loyalty - may have exaggerated his cousin's insensitivity towards Caroline, it was still difficult. She felt varying loyalties towards all of them. Lucas had clearly loved Caroline very dearly, as family, or he wouldn't have been so persistent in this mission. But telling him would be a betrayal of Caroline's memory. Jayne also felt a surge of guilt for having personally enjoyed his company so much, and she wasn't sure whether this was more on behalf of Victoria or Caroline. Ultimately she had promised Harry to keep quiet.

There was simply nothing to do except bite her tongue and try to bury what she had been told. When she was more settled, she could face Lucas again.

That encounter was going to be earlier than anticipated. When Jayne arrived at Aubrey's, where she was still staying, an invitation awaited. Aubrey had insisted on both her and Margaret Cade staying with him until Cade was fully recovered and able to go home. Now, as she came through the door, he instructed her to "Go and pack a weekend bag, we're off to the country."

"I can't possibly," Jayne said. "What about Cade?"

"It's frightful timing I know," Aubrey said, "But this is for Caroline. And Francis has his mother here. Besides, everyone is going." The word "everyone" had special emphasis.

"Who is everyone? And what is this about?"

"Everyone is all of us. Well, all except Francis of course. Even the rugged Rory, returned from far flung Peru or Patagonia or wherever he spends his days." Aubrey looked at Jayne slyly.

"But to what? What is the occasion?"

"It's a memorial tree planting for Caroline. An oak tree, in the grounds of her home. The handsome cousin rang me. He's been trying to get hold of you, by the way." Aubrey looked at her searchingly. He was too tactful to press her further, unlike Cade who would have tried to extract every last detail.

"It's strictly no black," Aubrey advised her as she went to pack. "The family want to celebrate Caroline's life, not repeat the funeral."

They must never, ever know what really happened, thought Jayne. Harry and I must take it to the grave. And she would have to confront Lucas. She hoped again that Cade's plight would buy her a bit more time.

"You've changed," said Aubrey, as they stood outside, trying to hail a cab to the station.

Jayne frowned. "I put on a coat as the evenings are drawing in, that's all."

"I didn't mean your clothes, I meant you. You're different somehow."

She felt a slight sense of panic. Was it obvious that she was hiding something, the news about Caroline?

"I've noticed it since you came back from Greece. My first impression was that you'd changed your hair, but it's more intrinsic than that."

"It can't be my tan," Jayne said lightly, "that faded almost immediately."

"Something happened there, something happened to you. I expect Francis would normally lend an ear. Please know that I will step up in his place, should you need me."

"Thank you Aubrey." She was very touched.

Harry's confession was weighing on her mind so much that she had barely had a moment spare to think about Rory. She hadn't seen him since graduation. He had fortunately had no idea of her unrequited feelings, and Jayne intended it to stay that way. How she would actually feel, when she saw him, was another matter.

They didn't see any of the others on the train, even though nearly everyone was coming up from London. It was an uneventful journey. Jayne tried to read, but was lost in her own thoughts, and Aubrey worked his way through the Times crossword, occasionally thinking aloud. Cade's presence was missed by both of them.

Lucas met them at the station to drive them to the house. Jayne felt a thrill of nerves when she saw him, and tried to affect tiredness to evade any questions. Hopefully Victoria would keep him occupied.

Just two weeks ago they had gathered here after Caroline's funeral. It already felt like months ago. Yet the sense of her death was still so present, almost unbelievable still. When would that eventually feel like long ago?

Jayne's room looked across the back of the house, over fields to low, rolling hills. It was such a beautiful part of the country here. Caroline had always spoken glowingly of her home. But the upkeep, repairs and maintenance were an ongoing worry. She remembered Lucas mentioning something about Caroline's plans to create a convalescent home. Would Harry continue with those ideas?

Something was niggling her. There was something she'd missed. When she tried to bring it to the top of her mind, all she remembered was sitting with Caroline in her rooms at university once, having tea and toast. Jayne remembered a painting of Caroline's home on the wall, which she had admired. Why did she remember this? What did Caroline say? Perhaps it would come to her in the middle of the night as these things tended to.

A gong sounded - an actual gong! - which must be the summons for supper. For a moment Jayne imagined butlers and footmen and a full complement of parlourmaids, but this was no longer the 1800s and the household was run along far leaner lines these days. There was a woman employed as a sort of cook-come-housekeeper, with a niece who helped out for larger functions, but beyond that Caroline's parents opened their own doors and swept their own floors.

And there, standing by the empty fireplace and looking rather lost, was Rory. It was a meeting that Jayne had anticipated for years. She had secretly rehearsed several different conversations, wondering if she could pluck up the courage urged by Cade to be a little more forward.

Instead she suddenly, finally saw him through Cade's eyes. Rory was less an idol deserving of worship than a huge, freckled, overgrown puppy. The hopeless-around-women persona that had seemed so endearing, and a useful excuse for her failure to connect with him, now seemed simply gauche and inept.

Despite the disappointment - or was it relief? - Jayne was still delighted to see him after so long, and greeted him warmly.

"Gosh Jayne, you're looking very well," Rory said. He also appeared to be seeing her with new eyes. "Whatever you've been up to must agree with you."

"You too. Always jetting off to foreign climes - it must be very exciting." Did her voice sound flat? She was trying to be enthusiastic. But over the years she had built him up into some kind of unattainable idol, and now he was no idol nor necessarily unattainable. The room, the light, the ambience were all flat.

Meanwhile Rory was grinning rather inanely. Jayne recognised the look. It was how he acted around the predatory Sloanes that spent their university years studying how to hook him. Oh, what a terrible irony it would be if he now started to feel what she no longer did!

It was a great relief when Lucy and Amanda joined them. Lucy, as sweet as ever in white, and Amanda in typically conservative blue. Rory and Lucy, that would be a perfect combination, Jayne thought, particularly after her broken engagement with John. She couldn't imagine Amanda getting married or even dating anyone. She never seemed to have had romantic involvements at university, nor expressed any interest in such.

"Hello Jayne," Lucy said. "Isn't this sad but such a lovely idea? Except for Cade not being here of course. How is he? Is there any improvement?"

Jayne answered as best she could.

"We discussed it, and thought it was best not to give the full details to Caroline's family," Amanda said. "We've just told them that Cade is unwell. It just seemed a bit stark to go into serious accidents and comas, given the circumstances."

Jayne appreciated the logic, though she privately hoped that Caroline's parents wouldn't ill judge Cade for not having managed to attend, if they were under the assumption that he was suffering from nothing more than a bad cold.

"I should mention that Harry does know," Jayne said. "I bumped into him outside Cade's place, so I had to tell him." Her mind went back to Harry's shocking, disturbing revelations.

"What was he doing outside Cade's place?" Amanda asked. "Do they know one another?"

"I didn't even think to ask."

Amanda turned her attention to Rory. "So you've finally returned to us," she said. "How long are you here for this time?"

"Indefinitely if I want, they've offered me a desk job. Don't think it's my thing though. I'll stick it out until the new year, then see. And how are you all doing?"

"Westminster is Westminster," Amanda said. "Nothing to report there. Lucy has recently been promoted, to Classical and Western Asiatic Antiquities nonetheless." Lucy blushed. "John I'm sure you have heard from, but he's well. Cade was recently written up in the Telegraph, and Aubrey is forever Aubrey. Still at the BBC."

Rory turned to Jayne. "And what about you, Jayne?"

"Just living very quietly."

"Hardly what I hear from Aubrey," Amanda said. "According to him you've been tearing all over the continent with Caroline's devastatingly handsome cousin."

Just at that moment Lucas appeared. Jayne wished she could close her eyes and just disappear. Fortunately Lucas, if he had heard - and surely he must have done - made no comment. He greeted them and introduced himself. Jayne couldn't bring herself to look him in the eye. Nor could she face looking at Rory. She looked at Lucy instead, who was blushing even more furiously.

Amanda was as supremely calm and self-possessed as ever. She chatted to Lucas about the house, about Cade's "flu", not knowing that he knew about the accident, leaving Jayne longing for the second gong.

Finally everyone was seated, and a pleasant if subdued dinner ensued. It could so easily have been an ordeal, but Lucas in particular worked hard to encourage a relaxed and companionable evening. Jayne was supposed to have been seated by him, but Rory had somehow taken his place, due to Aubrey arranging to sit near Caroline's father. He wanted to talk antiques. Or he wanted to meddle, Jayne thought uncharitably.

Harry, Victoria and John weren't there, they were all motoring up early the next morning. Given the tensions between Harry and Lucas at the lunch a few weeks ago, and her own recent encounter with Harry, it was for the best.

Rory was very attentive to Jayne throughout the meal, and she wrestled with herself not to find him irritating. There were only so many times she could decline the salt or pepper, or a refill of water, without wanting to snap. Lucy sat on his other side, and Aubrey, sitting on Lucy's left, had to compensate for Rory's neglect.

What has come over me? Jayne thought. She had spent years adoring this man and now he just annoyed her. Was part of her annoyance due to her former adoration, the realisation of the emotional energy and time wasted on him? If so it was hardly Rory's fault. She tried to be kinder, but that ran the risk of encouraging him. Poor Rory, having his *coup de foudre* half a decade too late.

Aubrey and Rory weren't the only ones who perceived a difference in Jayne. Lucy picked up on it as they had coffee afterwards. It was such a mild night that they had taken it outside, along the balustrade. Lucas, Rory and Amanda has gone on a moonlight stroll to spot an enormous badger that had allegedly been seen several times in the grounds. Jayne had declined, and Lucy had tactfully chosen to stay with her.

"Are you alright, Jayne?" Lucy asked. "Forgive me if I'm prying, but you seem unhappy, and not quite yourself."

Jayne attributed it to her worries over Cade, which Lucy accepted.

"Something about you is different though," Lucy said. "It's funny, when I saw you at the funeral I thought how lovely that you were exactly as you used to be at university, as though not a day had passed. And now, while of course you're no less lovely, you've changed. You would tell me, or Amanda, if there was a problem, wouldn't you? I know you're close to Cade, but I'd like to think you could turn to us as well."

Jayne thanked her, offering likewise. What she really longed for was sleep. A long, dreamless sleep.

15

The next day dawned cold and clear. The London latecomers arrived during breakfast. They heard Harry's car pull up on the gravel outside. Breakfast was quite a grand affair, with various silver tureens, wasted on Jayne who could never manage much more than coffee and toast at this hour.

John was his usual suave, impenetrable self. Jayne had always considered him rather a strange match for Lucy, too dry perhaps. His arrival didn't seem to cause Lucy any consternation; Jayne wondered at the exact circumstances of their break up. Everyone had made an effort to put a little colour into their costume but John wore city grey from head to foot. "He may as well have worn his horsehair," Aubrey said.

Harry seemed somewhat larger-than-life that morning. The round schoolboy face looked more incongruous than ever on his fairly tall frame, and his need for a haircut was growing daily. He appeared to have taken it upon himself to escort Victoria around. Jayne wondered if it was deliberately to rile Lucas. Victoria also showed very little affection towards Lucas.

Amanda had been surprised when Jayne mentioned that Victoria was Lucas' fiancée. "I hadn't realised," Amanda said. "From the way she conducts herself, anyone would think she was very much a single girl. She's practically in Harry's pocket." Making it worse, Jayne noticed that Harry rather shied away from Victoria whenever she, Jayne, was on the scene. He must have feared her disapproval, or perhaps was worried that she would reveal his story.

Shortly before they went down to the lake for the tree planting, John called Jayne into a side room, which turned out to be a small library dedicated to horticultural tomes, opening onto a conservatory. What a lovely room, she thought.

"I heard about Cade, of course," John said. "But there's something else. He's apparently been meddling in things that don't concern him. Whatever else, you must get him to stop. It's potentially dangerous."

A chill ran down Jayne's spine. "Do you have some sort of proof that the accident wasn't accidental?" she asked.

"Hardly. But if he keeps meddling it could put lives at risk. When you next see him, you might like to warn him."

"I can certainly mention it. I'm not sure what he would have been meddling in, though."

"Thank you," John said brusquely, closing the conversation. He would not mention it again, Jayne thought. John was efficient like that.

How strange. Why wouldn't John tell Cade directly? Jayne supposed she was viewed as Cade's closest friend, which must be why she was seen as the obvious go-to for this sensitive matter.

They were planting the oak tree on an island at the centre of the lake. It was a lovely place with willows at one end, and water fowl nesting. Apparently it had been one of Caroline's favourite spots. Once again Jayne felt almost nauseous at the loss of their friend, cheated out of so many years of happy and productive life. Yet she hadn't been happy, had she? And Lucas, currently talking with Victoria and Harry, was apparently the cause.

"I rather imagined us rowing over to the island on little boats," Lucy said. "The bridge came as a surprise."

"They should remove it afterwards," Victoria said, joining them. "Leave Caroline's tree in peace, visited only by ducks."

The way she phrased it came across as unfortunately flippant and needled Amanda. Unhappily for Victoria, she was the kind of girl that Amanda couldn't stand, and when Amanda disliked someone she became even more forthright than usual. Amanda didn't care a jot about people's private behaviour or any liaison Victoria may be having, but she did not suffer fools at all, let alone gladly.

"I should think that would be a bloody pointless idea," Amanda said. "I am sure Caroline's family would love to visit the tree, and sit there and think of her, as we all would. Her mother said they're planning to put a carved stone seat there when the tree is more established."

They stood around while the sapling was placed in the earth. A hole had already been dug. There was tenderness in the way Caroline's mother packed the soil around it, giving it support.

Edward Turbeville

Lucas had quoted Tennyson at Caroline's funeral. There had been drizzling grey rain outside the church, and when he had reached the line *"on the bald street breaks the blank day"* people had openly wept.

Now he quoted Tennyson again, but far happier verses:

"And long by the garden lake I stood
"For I heard your rivulet fall
"From the lake to the meadow and on to the wood
"Our wood, that is dearer than all."

He really did love her, Jayne thought. Whatever Harry's accusations, his interpretation of Lucas's behaviour towards Caroline must be wrong. If Lucas had caused his cousin pain, if there was unrequited love, it was not knowingly so.

They had been invited to spend the rest of the day and night there. Lucas urged them all to accept. "My aunt and uncle wish this to be as happy an occasion as possible despite the circumstances. They don't want people to be sadly slinking away immediately afterwards."

So it was agreed. Jayne and Aubrey went to telephone Mrs Cade. According to the doctors things were no better and no worse, but she felt quite strongly herself that there was an improvement. "I feel that Francis heard me when I spoke. Yesterday he seemed in a deeper sleep. He'll come back when he's ready," she said. Even over the phone she sounded happier and less anxious.

"I wouldn't be at all surprised if she were right," Aubrey said. "A mother's instinct. My own mother still rings me up if she senses I'm having a gloomy day, and she has not thus far wasted a call."

"You never seem gloomy, Aubrey," Jayne said. "Pensive sometimes, and even a little sad, but not gloomy." Aubrey always found some kind of silver lining amid disaster.

"The boy Rory is back with us for good, it would seem," Aubrey said. "The wanderlust has finally abandoned him, has it?" He eyed Jayne keenly.

"That was over very long ago," Jayne said. "Things are quite different now."

"Alas, must I pack my wedding waistcoat away yet again, and let the moths once more feast upon it?"

"You do that. And for heaven's sake don't try any more machinations at the lunch table."

16

They had promised to catch up for a "ladies' lunch" many times, and now when they finally met it would be as three instead of four. We leave so many things too late, but it used to feel like we had forever, Jayne thought as she waited for Lucy to arrive. She was meeting Jayne at Aubrey's first as she had an earlier appointment nearby. They could then travel together to the restaurant.

"Isn't Aubrey's flat wonderful!" Lucy said, as she put her umbrella into a carved Victorian stand, and entered the drawing room. "It's as big as a house! Good god, is that Ming?" She browsed around the rooms, looking at Aubrey's many treasures. It was an eclectic collection, ranging from Roman artefacts to Victoriana.

Jayne left Lucy to enjoy herself while she went and got a wrap. It was a windy, rainy day. When she came back from her room, Lucy was studying a marble bust.

"Hasn't Aubrey shown you his collection before?" Jayne asked.

"No, there always seemed to be something getting in the way. I was dying to see it, of course. This is the first time I've even been inside his flat, in fact."

They walked together through the drizzle of the day. The sky seemed to be brightening; it was less leaden than previously.

"Forgive me if I'm prying, Lucy, but I was sorry to hear about you and John, and I hope it wasn't too painful seeing him at the memorial," Jayne said.

"Not at all. The thing is that it was me who ended it. For some reason everyone thinks I'm the jilted fiancée. Though perhaps John let them think that, and if so I don't really mind, if it helps his pride."

Jayne was surprised, since that was certainly what most people, including herself, had thought.

"It sounds awful to say," Lucy said, "but I almost feel grateful for his mother being the straw that broke the camel's back."

"Really?"

"She's very religious, and John didn't want to upset her by us living together before we were married. I didn't mind that at all, since there's something rather exciting about the idea of moving in together for the first time after the wedding, isn't there? It's not as though one can't enjoy extended stays at one another's places beforehand.

"But it was holidays that started to irk me. John travels quite frequently, sometimes for cases or just a getaway, yet he would never invite me. I never knew where he was going from one week to the next. Eventually I tried to invite myself, whereupon he told me that it would really upset his mother to know that we were holidaying together unmarried. You know me, I don't like to lie, but I even suggested he fib and just not tell her.

"That made him irate for some reason, and then I suddenly decided I had had enough. It felt like he had some kind of double life that I wasn't part of. The thing is I don't think we were really in love any more. In fact I'm not sure we ever were," Lucy said.

"Surely at university, in the early days?" Jayne asked. "You were together for years, it must have meant something."

"I honestly think it did mean nothing. It was just too suitable and convenient at the time. He was always very considerate, of course, but shouldn't there be something more?"

Considerate did not sound like fireworks and shooting stars to Jayne. She thought of her own parents. Yes, they had been extremely considerate to one another, and very perceptive about one another's needs, but there was definitely more, even in their elderly years. Sometimes she wished they had gone at the same time, awful though it would have been for her to lose both parents at once, to spare her father those last lonely years living with the sad memories of his loss.

"I wonder whether we'll all be lucky enough to find it, if that is so," she said to Lucy.

They had reached the restaurant, a small bistro in Covent Garden. Amanda was already there.

"We've been discussing true love," Lucy told her. "And my break up with John."

"A far more happy event than your wedding would have been," Amanda said. "I was all set to wear black, and make an objection."

Jayne hadn't realised that Amanda disliked John, and said so.

"Did any of us really like him?" Amanda said. "Sorry, Lucy, but I must be honest." It was rare for Amanda to apologise for her opinion. "We put up with him because he roomed with Rory. And they did throw some wonderful parties. But beyond that, he was never really one of us, was he?

"Now hurry and take a look through the menu because I've been here for nearly twenty minutes and I'm starving."

Inspired by hunger and the menu, they spent the first half hour discussing food and new restaurants.

"If I had time to eat out every night I would be as fat as butter," Amanda said.

"Are your hours quite long?"

"Not officially, but we've had some large projects on in recent months, and there's been a considerable amount of candle burning." She turned to Jayne. "Now what about you, what are your plans now?"

"My plans?" Jayne asked, confused.

"Now you're finally out of hibernation. Will you be moving up here? And what do you plan to do?"

"I wasn't in hibernation," Jayne said.

Amanda put down her fork and looked at her very directly. "You went into retirement. There's no other way to put it. At a time when everyone else was starting out in the world, you hung up your boots and became a leisurely spinster of the parish at the age of twenty-one. It's obscene."

Jayne didn't want to use her father's death as an excuse, though that was the main reason for her initial withdrawal. Despite it being an anticipated event, nothing had prepared her for the aftermath: the sheer, stark loneliness, the isolation. Worse even than her mother's death, for now she had no one.

"It was always a bit different, with my parents being older," Jayne said. Even though they both could and should have lived a good few years longer, she thought, particularly her mother. It was the bitterness that lingered, the sense of unfairness at a premature parting. She had sensed the same for Caroline's parents; it was unbearable to lose someone before their time.

"Were they so much older?" Lucy asked. "How old was your mother when she had you?"

Jayne's parents had tried for many years to start a family, but the blessing had not happened. After nearly thirty years of marriage they hardly expected it to. They had given up, with great sadness, and thrown their energies into other things: charitable work, the garden, literary pursuits. Tiny little gowns her mother had embroidered in the hopeful, early days of her marriage were wrapped in tissue paper and tucked away in drawers, to yellow over the years.

Then, on the eve of her forty-ninth birthday, what was understandably thought to be menopause turned out to be something quite different. At an age where they had expected to become grandparents, Jayne's parents bore their first and only child.

"She was forty-nine when I arrived," Jayne said. "Nearly seventy when she died. My father was a few years older than her, and in his eighties."

"I am sorry, Jayne," Lucy said. "I take it for granted that my family is just there."

"I had them both into adulthood, that's more than some people get. Consider Cade." Cade's father had died when he was very young.

"Talking of Cade," said Amanda, "I thought we might visit him this afternoon, if you think it won't be too much."

Jayne said it would be fine. They picked up some flowers and some sandwiches for Mrs Cade on their way to the Tube. She continued to insist on keeping vigil for all the visitor hours allowed, in case he woke.

Cade looked very pale, but Jayne thought she could see what his mother meant about his improving. He seemed to be more present somehow, sleeping rather than comatose.

"He seems a bit nearer the surface than when I saw him a few days ago," Lucy said, which described it well.

"His eyelids have been flickering," Margaret Cade told them, "and he sometimes gives a slight pressure of his hand."

There was renewed hope once more.

17

Jayne was startled by a knock at the door not long after she arrived back at Aubrey's Bloomsbury flat. He was on yet another trip, Margaret Cade was still keeping vigil at the hospital, and no one was expected.

Feeling oddly nervous, wary even, she went to open the door. She wasn't sure whether she was relieved or not to see that it was Rory. Had it been anyone else she would have felt pleased to see them, as the flat seemed so cavernous when she was alone there. With Rory she felt awkward.

"Hello," he said. "I expect I should have called first, but I'm useless with numbers. I couldn't even remember the address, but fortunately it's on the end of the row."

Jayne was just about to offer him a drink when the phone rang. It was Lucas.

"Jayne, finally! I've been trying to get hold of you for days."

"I am sorry, Lucas, but would you mind if I called you back later? A friend has just dropped by this very minute."

"Certainly." There wasn't a lot else he could say.

Jayne knew that she would have to face him at some point. "Will you be in town again soon?"

"I'll be up in a few days. Let's have lunch," Lucas suggested.

"That would be lovely." She hoped she sounded sincere. She wasn't sure whether she was or not. Part of her longed to see him, but Harry's revelations couldn't be ignored.

Rory was hovering in the doorway. "Do come in," Jayne said. "Have a seat. What can I get you?"

"Oh, anything's fine." It was a useless answer.

"Tea then?" She boiled the kettle and got out what she hoped was Aubrey's least valuable tea set. Jayne was not particularly clumsy by nature, but eighteenth century porcelain was enough to give anyone tremors.

"Milk? Sugar?" Everything felt so very odd and uncomfortable. Perhaps she should have opened up Aubrey's drinks cabinet.

Rory sat on the sofa, across from her, looking rather ill at ease and even gangly. She noticed that he'd dropped a lot of the solidness from his university days. "Are you still playing rugby?" she asked.

"Not really. It's too hard with living overseas. Cricket's somewhat easier."

Rory's Sloanes would have known the right things to say, to butter him up and keep light conversation going. Jayne simply found it too much effort.

"So tell me about some of the countries you've been in? Did someone mention Peru?"

"Not Peru, no. Mainly Africa."

"Did you enjoy it?"

"It wasn't too bad."

This was hopeless. Just as she was mentally flailing around for something to say, Rory let her off the hook.

"I heard you went to Greece."

"Yes, on holiday with some cousins of mine. They're keen sailors. I enjoyed the scenery more than the sea."

"Lots of ruins?" Rory asked.

"Yes, they were spectacular. We were staying near Delphi, where the Oracle of Apollo used to be."

"John mentioned you went back again."

Jayne realised Rory was digging around rather ineptly, trying to bring up an awkward subject. Then he blurted out:

"Do you think there was something wrong with Caroline's death? Is that why you went?"

Jayne was at a loss as to how to respond. Honesty seemed easiest. "Yes. There were just some things we wanted to check over, and going there felt a little like paying tribute."

"Someone said you thought you saw Caroline, after she was supposed to be dead?"

She fell back on Cade's original suggestion. "I think what really happened is that I glimpsed her a couple of weeks before, and then the memory of that got suppressed, and then I saw someone else who superficially resembled her."

Rory didn't look as though he really followed. Although he must have passed some exams to get to university, he had never seemed the brightest of the bunch. Even when Jayne's feelings for him were at their height she had been forced to admit this to herself.

"What I was thinking, Jayne, is that if you needed me to do anything, I'd be very happy to try. I've spent the past few years dealing with foreign officials and locals in different places, and one gets used to the processes."

"Everything's pretty much complete now, but thank you."

"So you won't be going back to Greece again to investigate any further?"

"I have no plans to, no." She couldn't speak for Lucas.

"That's alright then," Rory said. "Just let me know if you are, though." He sat up a little straighter. "On another matter, I was rather wondering if you might like to have dinner with me one evening?"

Just as she had thought she was off the hook! And why did it trouble her so much? He didn't know the strength of her former feelings, nor that they had gone. Perhaps she could go out with him just as old friends, and even have an enjoyable night.

"That would be lovely, Rory, thank you. Just so long as there are no misunderstandings. The thing is, until quite recently, there was someone. Very recently in fact. So the timing isn't quite right for anything else just as yet."

If he was disappointed he masked it well.

"Perhaps let's wait until Cade has recovered," Jayne said. "Everything will be easier then."

18

There was wonderful news the next day: Cade had finally come round. He had opened his eyes, spoken, and even managed some hospital tea. He had no memory of the accident according to his mother, and had been unable to help the police.

Jayne rushed over around the middle of the morning, to find Margaret Cade holding her son's hand and talking happily with him. Jayne had brought the latest edition of The Stage as well as a huge bunch of grapes.

He was still very pale and weak, but everything was getting back to normal.

Cade sent his mother off to get him a coffee so he could speak alone with Jayne.

"It's funny, I remember nothing of the accident, but I do remember needing to talk with you, and fortunately what about. It's as though the only things erased are from mid-morning on the day of the accident to now. Makes you wonder how the brain stores memories, for there to be such a sharp cut off," he said.

He asked after the others. Jayne was able to report that everyone was well, though when she got to Rory her composure faltered slightly.

"There's something going on there, isn't there Jayne? No, don't deny it, it's all over your face. Don't tell me that Rugby Boy has finally come back from Brunei with a brain cell? He's asked you out, hasn't he?"

Jayne gave him a brief account of how things stood.

Cade started laughing. "Years and years you waste longing for that freckled fool. When he finally puts himself on a platter, you're not only disinterested but actively annoyed with him?"

"Not annoyed, perhaps more frustrated with myself, or the timing."

"I'd also like to register an objection to you using my near-death experience to escape your own near-death experience. For I can't imagine anything more deadly dull than a liaison with Rory."

"Aubrey didn't seem to think so. He kept swapping the seating around at Caroline's house. I wish you had been there for the memorial," Jayne said. "It was sad, of course, but it was also lovely, and peaceful."

"On that subject," Cade said, "I have something very interesting to tell you. Thank God my longer-term memory does not appear to have been affected. Let me begin at the beginning."

And Cade told Caroline what he had discovered. Since his first conversation with Jayne about Caroline's secret service summoning, he had become fascinated with the notion and process of recruitment. "I'm not sure why. I partly wondered if it might be a good idea for a play. But mainly I wanted to be sure."

Cade had travelled to their old college to seek out their former tutor, Professor Chetwynd.

"It actually went very well. He seemed to be extremely flattered about my name change. I had been worrying about that point," Cade said, "because a theatrical connotation is not for everyone."

"I shouldn't think he would have to worry about that for a few years yet," Jayne said. "Far more likely that people will wonder if that obscure actor is related to the highly esteemed academic and well known author, than the other way around."

"You wound me," said Cade, "and I am under strict instructions not to be upset or excited. However, before you cause me to have a relapse, let me continue my tale."

He closed his eyes for a moment, and Jayne was worried he was exhausting himself. But she let him carry on.

"I passed on the sad news about Caroline. I mentioned her profession as a sort of open secret. 'Of course,' I said, 'given Caroline's work, one accepts that there may be risk.' It was apparently news to Chetwynd that she had taken the route she did. He clearly doesn't follow up on the people he sends on."

"That might be wise, given the secrecy. Safer for him perhaps," Jayne said.

"Yes. So we'd had some of his sherry - god it took me back - and I managed to chat about something else, the state of the Telegraph's book reviews, or that kind of thing, making sure he'd finished a second glass at least. He always gave far more amusing tutorials after he'd had a couple. Anyway it was a successful strategy, because when I mentioned Professor Plum - I picked a name out at random, one of the history professors at a neighbouring college - he was only too delighted to correct me and inadvertently reveal the real name."

"Who is he?"

"Quite a disappointment, really. I had built up hopes by then that it might even be the Chancellor." Cade gave her the name of a professor of Ancient Greek, notable in his field but otherwise obscure.

"Ancient Greek of all things."

"An odd coincidence - nothing more though I should think. More frustratingly, he had retired a couple of years ago. I had to track him down in some elderly people's home in the West country. He was past eighty when he officially retired," Cade said. "Though I think he had quit teaching some time before."

They were interrupted by the return of Mrs Cade. Jayne was frustrated but relieved at the same time. Cade really did need to take things very carefully right now, the rest of the details could wait.

The British Museum was only a short walk from Aubrey's flat. Jayne felt a thirst to be somewhere calm and orderly, as removed from the bustle of the modern world as it was possible to be in London.

Her trips to Greece swayed her towards the Graeco-Roman antiquities. She found herself in the quiet symmetry of the Duveen Gallery, stark and still against the detail and vitality of the Elgin Marbles. As she wandered through the room she thought of Delphi. The contrast between the sculptures here, preserved in their cool mausoleum, and the still crumbling temples, weathered by the sun, wind and rain.

What struck Jayne was how familiar a couple of artefacts looked. A marble panel of charioteers, and the bronze statuette of a huntsman, naked except for a cape. The bronze was so flawless it seemed eerily modern, but its face was the face of antiquity. Did people look like that? Jayne wondered. Do we still look like that?

She hadn't spent much time in museums during her time in Greece, preferring to remain outdoors and visit actual sites and structures, rather the treasures stripped from them. Why did she feel like it was only yesterday that she had looked at something just like this centaur, locked forever in balletic conflict with a cloaked warrior, his head long broken away and lost?

As she sat contemplating the marble bust of an unknown man, she remembered where. Aubrey's flat. In his study there was a sculpture mounted on the wall, very similar to the Elgin Marble panel, carved with a centaur and a similar warrior, in a different pose. Very expensive even as a replica, Jayne thought.

Something lingered though, at the back of her mind. Something unsettled. She needed to finish her conversation with Cade of course. Hopefully he would have managed some lunch, and be rested by the afternoon visiting hours.

19

"So where did I get up to?" Cade asked. It was the afternoon, and after enduring a barrage of tests and hospital food, he had been allowed visitors again. Mrs Cade had hurried home to prepare Cade's flat, as the doctors indicated a release sooner than later, barring no further complications.

"You had tracked down Professor Plum, to a nursing home in the West country."

"That's it. More of a retirement home, there weren't too many nurses anyway. Most of the inmates seemed perfectly *compos mentis*. Plum, as we'll continue to call him, also appeared satisfactorily lucid. The problem was - and perhaps this happens to everyone as they get older - that time seems to become less sequential. There's so much of it, so many memories, that you run them all together simultaneously. So he remembered certain events well, but they were superimposed by other things from other times. It was fascinating, and rather sad."

"Did he remember Caroline? How did you introduce yourself?" Jayne asked.

"I started with a little white lie and mentioned that I was Caroline's cousin. I thought that might be safer and easier than claiming to be an old friend. I told him that she had died, and he said he was very sorry, and I believe he was. I doubt it's the first time he's had such news, sending people off to high risk work as he does. Even though his role is minor, he's still part of the process."

Cade sipped a little water. His hand was rather unsteady. Caroline thought privately that it was unlikely the doctors would just let him walk out of there within the next twenty-four hours.

"This is where it gets interesting. I mentioned knowledge of his introduction, for want of a better word, and some burble about Caroline always being dedicated to serving her country. I hoped it might make the eyes a little more misty and it did. Besides it wasn't even a lie, she used to collect for old soldiers on Remembrance Day, if you recall, and I'm sure she once told me she would like to open a veterans' hospital. I always thought it was rather Lady of the Manor, but perhaps that was unfair of me.

"Anyway, I digress. Plum became a little mistier, as I mentioned, and began to reminisce. And he said 'I remember there were two of them that year, quite remarkable'. I pushed him to explain, and he said that Caroline was one of two students he had sent through, from Chetwynd. It was only every few years he found a suitable candidate, and here were two from the same college and the same discipline.

"I tried to verify everything as thoroughly as I could. I thought it was possible he confused the date, but he was convinced of his dates and started talking about a sinking in the Boat Race that year. We could always check that as well, though I haven't had a chance to yet. I also thought to ask if Chetwynd definitely only sent potential candidates from his own tutor group - which would be the eight of us - and this apparently was the case."

Cade looked at Jayne while she absorbed what he had said.

"So you mean that another one of the set is also working for MI6?"

"It would seem so," he said. "Obviously I had a photo of Caroline with me, and it was a copy of that group shot of all of us, on Finals morning, all dressed up ready for exams and looking pretty grim. So I showed him the other faces. But he didn't recognise any of them, not even her."

"Do you think that this second agent has a bearing on what happened to Caroline?" Jayne asked.

"I'm not sure. But it's rather odd, isn't it? Another one of the eight is involved in intelligence work, and we have no idea who."

"In fairness, I didn't have any idea about Caroline before you enlightened me a few weeks ago. And we still have no actual proof," Jayne said.

"No, but it's shivery, isn't it? I wonder who it is. I'm inclined to wonder if it might be you."

Jayne told him not to be so absurd.

"But think about it," he said. "It's likely to be someone who is overseas a lot."

"Not necessarily."

"Well let's suppose it is. You live by yourself down in Little Villagebury-Under-Hill, fairly secretively and mysteriously, no one would have a clue about how many times you might actually be popping over to the continent. Perhaps you tell the neighbour, when you hand her your cat to look after, that you're just going to visit an old aunt in Norfolk. Then you jet off overseas on yet another secret mission."

"Don't be ridiculous. I don't even have a cat."

"But by the far most telling point," Cade said, ignoring her, "is that you were in Greece when it all happened. And jetted back there soon afterwards."

"It would make my subsequent investigations rather absurd though, wouldn't it? Unless I was playing a truly bizarre game of double bluff."

"So you're saying it is you?"

"I can't believe you're serious! Are you really asking me if I work for MI6?!"

"Caroline clearly did," said Cade. "It's not much of a stretch to wonder if you were the other recruit."

Jayne still wasn't sure if Cade was being serious or not. He had had a long time to think about this. "I can tell you honestly and sincerely that I do not and have never worked for the secret service," she said. "I can't prove a negative, though you're welcome to look through my handbag for government cards or a diplomatic passport, or whatever they may carry."

"So who is it then?"

It could pretty much have been any of them, Jayne thought: Amanda, Lucy, Rory, John or Aubrey. Even Cade, she supposed. Though his telling her of the agent's existence rather ruled him out. Unless he was the one contriving an elaborate double bluff.

"Let's go through everyone," Cade said. "We've already detailed the reasons for and against it being you, and we know Caroline was the first agent. In the spirit of fair play, I'll let you include me as well."

Jayne realised he was indeed serious. "This isn't a game for you, is it? You actually have a hunch?" Then she suddenly remembered John's bizarre warning. Did this mean John was the second agent, or perhaps knew who was? If sinister business was afoot, then Caroline had had an enemy, and so did anyone else poking around.

There was no way she could tell Cade about her encounter with John. Yet, anyway. He was already worked up over his discovery, and the doctors had specified he needed to stay as calm and unstressed as possible.

"Number One: Lucy. Always very sweet, that could just be an act. Has a job that enables a lot of travel."

"She also recently got promoted to covering Classical antiquities, if you want to throw that into the pot," Jayne said. "It would certainly facilitate travel to countries such as Greece and Italy, and the fringes of Eastern Europe."

Cade continued his analysis. "Split up with her fiancé recently. I'm not sure how that's relevant, but I will add it to my mental notebook."

"Number Two: Amanda. Terrifyingly capable. Works in Westminster which is easy and convenient on many levels. No one has ever known anything about her private life. Could defend herself in any situation armed with just a hockey stick. No - I'm not joking - they don't just drop the weak and useless into high risk locations. You'd have to be capable of defending yourself in a sticky situation. Amanda would have been a perfect recruit for that. Give her a gold star in your mind."

"You've watched far too many spy films," Jayne said. But she played along. "Number Three can be me, and we needn't go over that again. In short, I live a remote and mysterious life, and I was in Greece when Caroline died. Quite what my interest would be in stirring up a hornets' nest, which is essentially what I've done, I'll leave it to your fertile imagination to invent."

"Number Four, Caroline. The first recruit," Cade said.

"Number Five: Aubrey. A man of extensive means and contacts. Travels regularly all over the world, particularly to Europe, in the pursuit of antiques. Which would be an easy cover for some other kind of work."

Jayne thought of all the artefacts at Aubrey's mansion flat. An exceedingly expensive cover, if that really were the case.

"I just cannot imagine it's Aubrey," Jayne said. "If it is, then he certainly had nothing to do with any of this." She had seen Aubrey's reaction after Cade was hurt. If John's warning could be taken to mean that the car accident may have been a deliberate hit, then Aubrey could have had nothing to do with the matter.

"Number Six: Cade, me. It's not me."

"That's hardly fair!"

"Alibis, my dear girl. I've been treading the boards at the Playhouse every night for weeks."

"Number Seven: John. A brilliant mind, used to talking or arguing his way through situations. Recent split with fiancée. I don't trust him and I've never thought he held many of us in particularly high esteem either. Put a gold star by his name."

Jayne added a second gold star to her mental list.

"Last but not least, Number Eight: Rory. Constantly overseas, which is a plus point; amiable plank which is a negative. Yes, it could be an act, but to my knowledge he's been that way since Freshers' Week. He's very athletic, so has the same advantage as Amanda in that regard. I'm not inclined to waste a star on him though."

"Not even a silver star?"

"No. But you might put a silver star on Lucy. She surely can't be as sweet as she always seems."

20

The leaves were already changing on the plane trees in Berkley Square where Jayne sat on a bench, awaiting Lucy. She had chosen the location as it was a short walk from Lucy's office, and they should make the most of the early Autumn sunshine.

Jayne needed to talk to someone, and Lucy seemed safest. Though she didn't believe for a moment that Lucy deserved Cade's silver star of suspicion, she still planned to be circumspect.

She saw Lucy approaching, wearing a light grey coat, and waved to her.

As they made an informal picnic of sandwiches, Jayne mentioned her trip to the British Museum. "I hadn't been there in years," she said.

"I always find it rather overwhelming," Lucy said. "You can only see the barest fraction on any one visit, it's such a huge place. And did you know that at any one time only one per cent of the collection is on show?"

"It would take a lifetime to see it all."

"Certain artefacts can't be put on permanent display for conservation reasons," Lucy said. "I know it's horribly commercially minded of me, but sometimes I can't help wondering how much it would all fetch at auction. People pay the most outlandish amounts for even obscure, broken little pieces of this and that. And everything at the museum is so fine."

This seemed the ideal opening for Jayne to mention something that was still niggling at her mind. "Aubrey has some lovely pieces."

"Yes," said Lucy. Something in her voice caught Jayne's attention.

"I know Aubrey's quite wealthy," Jayne said, "but surely they would be replicas? He has a panel in his study which is just like one of the Elgin Marbles."

"I know the one you mean, one of the Metopes rather than the Frieze. A centaur and warrior."

"That's the one," Jayne said.

Lucy looked at her. "I studied it quite closely, before we went to lunch. It's certainly very convincing, for a replica."

"It must be a replica, aren't all the Elgin Marbles in the museum?"

Lucy shook her head. "No, there are quite a few missing. Many of the Southern ones - the Centauromachy with the centaurs on - were destroyed in the seventeenth century by a cannonball."

"How much would one of them be likely to go for at auction?"

"It's very hard to say since they never come up, for obvious reasons. Seven figures, certainly."

They were both silent for a while, watching people come and go, finishing their lunches, leaving crumbs for the birds, returning to their offices.

"Do you think you might stay up here in London?" Lucy asked.

"I did think so. I was even going to look for a job. But now I find I miss home more than I thought, and particularly the garden," Jayne said. "Before I thought I was continuing to tend it out of respect to my parents, but I realise I love it too, for myself."

"You've probably inherited some sort of green-fingered gene."

"I'm not terribly successful with new plants, it's more the appreciation of it that I've learned from them. Here," Jayne indicated the surrounding area, "there are beautiful parks, but hardly anyone has a decent sized garden. And I certainly wouldn't. My budget would barely meet the seediest of tiny flats."

"You could always room with us. We have a sort of box room, and we've discussed many times how nice a third girl would be," Lucy offered.

"Thank you, I'll certainly consider it."

They progressed to talking about Caroline, reminiscing about old times. And now we are seven, Jayne thought. She decided to take the plunge.

"You remember I mentioned how shortly before the memorial I encountered Harry in London?"

"Yes, you passed on the news about Cade. Thank goodness he's better, by the way," Lucy said.

"Harry told me something. The most extraordinary story. He swore me to secrecy, so I've kept my lip buttoned, but I'm no longer sure that his interpretation is correct."

"You've intrigued me now. If you want to tell me, I can be discreet."

Jayne related what she could about the awful mix up, and Caroline's alleged suicide attempts. She left out the allegations against Lucas. She no longer believed them anyway.

"None of that sounds in the least like Caroline," Lucy said. "But then I suppose one can never truly know what goes on in other people's lives."

"I thought so too. That's why I wanted someone else's perspective. What I'm wondering is whether it was an accident, made to look like suicide."

"You think Caroline was murdered?"

"I'm not sure. There is her secret service work, that may have put her at risk."

"I had heard something about that, but I was never quite sure how credible it was," Lucy said. "Poor Harry. I don't see how one could ever get over something like that. He must have been so close to bumping into her, talking to her, perhaps saving her. It's like missing someone stranded in the desert by a few yards."

"If she did go on to kill herself. If it was murder, then his presence there would probably not have mattered either way."

Lucy had finally joined the dots. "Of course, this means that you did see her, didn't you? No wonder you were so adamant and then so confused in the pub after the funeral. I'm so sorry for that."

"Don't be. It wasn't your fault at all."

"How did she look when you saw her?" Lucy asked.

"Certainly not suicidal. She was with several other people, all men. They looked like they had been diving, commercial diving perhaps. She walked quite close to me, she must have seen me as I called out to her. I suspect she couldn't blow her cover or something."

"Or perhaps she really didn't hear you," Lucy said. "She may have had ear plugs in, or perhaps they popped, and she was just absorbed in her own thoughts and didn't see you. If she was feeling depressed, she might have been in a bit of a fog."

Jayne thought that this was highly doubtful, but said nothing.

"One thing I do find odd is how quickly Harry went home. I should have thought he would have at least tried to have flown back with Caroline's body. Wouldn't that be the normal thing to do?" Jayne asked.

"He was in pretty bad shock though, and might just have wanted to get out of there and be with his family," Lucy said.

Jayne felt guilty after she arrived back at Aubrey's. He had been such a generous and thoughtful host, and here she was gossiping about his collection with Lucy. She studied the marble panel in question again, its figures frozen in an eternal battle. To her layman's eyes, she couldn't see how one would tell if it was real or a replica. Either way, carving such a work in modern times would still surely require a great deal of skill and expense.

Aubrey was due to return that evening, but he rang to say he was delayed and wouldn't be there until nearly midnight, so they should dine without him.

Margaret Cade and Jayne supped companionably. The older woman was transformed since Cade's recovery. She seemed ten years younger. How worry ages a person, Jayne thought. She remembered the grey look her father developed during her mother's illness that never quite went away, and then he began ailing himself and grew even greyer.

One thing was still troubling Margaret: "What about Francis's job? He's missed so many performances, do you think the theatre will have found someone else to take his place?"

Jayne explained to her about understudies and assured her that Cade would be fine.

"And what will you do? I feel sad for you all alone in that house, my dear, though I'm sure it's a lovely place. It can't be easy for you with both parents gone. I worry about what will happen to Francis when I go, with no brothers or sisters. I hope he settles down soon."

"What about cousins?" Jayne asked. "I think you mentioned you had a sister. Does she have children?"

"A sister and a brother. He has several cousins, yes, but it's not the same. I should have married again, I suppose. I was just too taken up in everything after Francis's father's death to even consider it. And as boys grow up, it becomes much harder for them to adapt to a stepfather. By then of course you're used to being by yourself, and having to deal with all a man's habits again would just be a nuisance."

Cade was due to leave hospital the next day. Margaret Cade packed up her things that evening so she could move herself to his flat in the morning.

As Cade only had one tiny spare bedroom, and his mother would probably want to make the most of her time with him before she went home, Jayne had decided to stay on at Aubrey's. She was longing to chat further with Cade about many things, but it would have to wait.

Jayne carried them both a cup of tea and some biscuits by the fire. It was only a gas fire - how she longed for her open log fire back home! - but it felt cosy and even decadent turning it on this early in the year. The night was the chilliest yet, a sign of summer's parting.

21

They enjoyed another one of Aubrey's leisurely breakfasts the next morning, which was a Saturday. Aubrey had arrived back very late, after they had gone to bed, and Jayne wasn't sure if he would be up much before noon. But there he was, in his imperial purple dressing gown, doing something marvellous with eggs.

"Mrs H won't let me touch a pan when she's around," Aubrey said, referring to his housekeeper. "My *cordon bleu* skills have developed in rebellion to her iron rule."

"She keeps a very tidy house," Margaret Cade said. She had been a little disconcerted by the presence of Mrs H, having anticipated doing some cooking and housework herself for Aubrey in recompense for his hospitality. Finding a highly capable, rather stately woman already keeping the rooms in a flawless condition had upset her plans. Jayne had assured her that Aubrey was only too happy to host her during Cade's hospitalisation, or at any other time, but Margaret Cade fretted privately about not being able to repay his kindness.

Edward Turbeville

Having finished her tea and Aubrey's omelette, she excused herself to go and finish putting her things together.

Jayne had first assumed that "Mrs H" stood for "Mrs Housekeeper", but on meeting the woman for the first time she had learnt that it was Mrs Honiton. The housekeeper appeared to have been bequeathed with the flat, having ministered to Aubrey's great uncle in previous years.

Aubrey had always been a neat person, and liked his own peace and quiet, and Jayne suspected that he kept Mrs II on more out of kindness than genuine need. A daily cleaner for a couple of hours a day would have been more than sufficient for him.

"My great uncle lunched at his club, and dined at home," Aubrey had explained. "I lunch at work and prefer to dine out. It has been rather problematic. In the end I compromised by yielding breakfasts to Mrs H, and insisting that she takes weekends off. Great-Uncle Charles had her for all intents and purposes enserfed for seven days. Fortunately she did not 'live in', that would have been a very awkward situation."

Jayne asked him how his latest trip had gone.

"A disappointment. A flight of fancy with not a fancy to be found."

Jayne commiserated.

"But perhaps there was one nugget," Aubrey said. "What's that phenomenon when you learn of something, then soon after hear about it again? Not déjà-vu. Is it synchronicity, perhaps?"

"I'm not sure. Perhaps if you explain what it was we'll manage to think of the term."

"Very well. I only recently learned, from our friend Francis, about our late friend Caroline's rather fascinating career. No doubt I should have guessed such, had my mind ever turned to the question, but I will confess that it came as a complete surprise." Aubrey took a piece of toast from an ornate silver rack, buttered it thickly, and reached for the marmalade.

"Imagine my surprise and consternation when only a short time later, a bizarre rumour reaches my ears, involving the secret service, and specifically operations in Greece. Apparently there is a brouhaha within the walls of Whitehall over leaked military secrets and possible high level defection across the Iron Curtain. Reports of double agents in the ranks."

Ideas began flying around in Jayne's mind. She needed time to pin them down, to get a better sense of the new shapes forming. "If you can bear with me, Aubrey, I think it's possible that your information could be very significant. There's a great deal I need to fill you in on, but I have to think about some things first. I'm not sure I can really explain everything now, but is there any way we could speak again with your contact?"

"Alas! I languish at the end of a lengthy chain of Chinese Whispers, all too far from the source," Aubrey said. "But I will see if the threads can be traced back. Your theory, of course, is that our friend discovered this treachery, or was perhaps sent to investigate it, and thereby met her doom? We must have all considered foul play, given her role there."

Jayne's thoughts had not quite crystallised to such an extent, but it did feel like she had been wandering through a dense, dark forest and finally there was the glimpse of a sunlit clearing ahead.

Before she could update Aubrey with Cade's revelation - and likewise she needed to let Cade know of this latest piece of information - Margaret Cade returned, ready to leave for the hospital. They were all going together to see the convalescent, and hopefully bring him home. Aubrey had insisted on hiring a taxi for the morning as he wanted Cade transported with as little disruption as possible. To allay Margaret's concerns about expense, Aubrey had lied and told her that the taxi driver was Mrs H's nephew.

"It was easier than claiming he was my cousin, and then having to go through a faux family conversation. This way I can legitimately pretend barely to know the fellow."

Jayne had a moment's pang of concern that the taxi driver might, based on his appearance, be very obviously not a relation of Mrs H, but he turned out to be an amiable east Londoner. If Margaret Cade thought it odd that the genteel Mrs H had a cockney cab-driving nephew, she did not say anything. Most likely she was too wrapped up in thoughts of Cade to even notice or question.

Operation Home Cade passed without issue, and they sat around Cade's flat while his mother bustled about in the kitchen, finally queen of her own domain. Inspired by Aubrey's jewel-hued robes she had bought Cade a new dressing gown to recuperate in. He sat, reluctantly draped in maroon velour, plied with soup and tea.

"I shall go mad," he said, lamenting. "She is the dearest woman, but by god! There are matching slippers."

Although it wasn't easy furthering their discussions with Cade's mother around, Cade pointed out that it didn't really matter if she overheard anything. "She won't have a clue what we're talking about, she'll probably think it's one of my plays," he said.

So Cade and Aubrey were both brought up to date with one another's discoveries: Cade's revelation, via Professor Plum, of the second recruit from their own ranks, and Aubrey's information, via his media contacts, about the suspected defection. Jayne felt uncomfortable about withholding Harry's confession over the mix-up and alleged suicide. Now that it seemed increasingly likely to her that Harry was mistaken, or had been deliberately led up the garden path for whatever reason, perhaps she should share it with them?

She was also keeping John's odd warning to herself. It didn't really tell them anything more, for now. Should it seem more important later on, she would of course mention it.

"Good lord," Cade said, as Aubrey finished his divulgement. "This has turned into a considerable intrigue."

Jayne made a decision. If she wanted their help, or rather if Lucas did, full disclosure was the only strategy.

"Actually there's more," she said. "Something I didn't tell either of you earlier, for which I'm sorry. But you'll understand why, I hope, when I do."

"Go on," said Aubrey.

"In brief: I met Harry shortly before the memorial. He told me the most extraordinary story about mixing up bodies at the hospital and Caroline allegedly attempting suicide twice. I was so shocked when he first related everything that I just did as he requested and kept quiet. But several things, including both of your revelations, have led me to believe that he was wrong, and that someone was deliberately misleading him. I also don't think it sounded like Caroline, like something she would do."

"You'd better give us the full details," Cade said, so Jayne recounted them as best she could.

"Not a chance Caroline would do such," Aubrey said. "That flop haired fool has scant appreciation of his own sister's mettle. Swallowing pills over a broken heart? I wouldn't even think that lowly of Lucy."

"Lucy is tougher than you think. I actually told her about Harry's story, because I needed some outside perspective. She found the notion of Caroline taking her own life just as absurd as you do."

"What about this second agent then?" Aubrey asked. "I can assure you it's not me."

Cade looked rather shamefaced. "Jayne and I made a sort of list," he said, "and starred the most likely suspects. Amanda and John were awarded gold stars, and Lucy a silver one. You'll be glad, perhaps, that we absolved you."

"I'm not glad at all. Clearly you fail to perceive the remotest jot of mystery or excitement about me. Far from picturing me with a secret life of intrepid intrigue and derring do, you cast me aside as safe and dull and utterly without mystique. And what is it with you and girls, Francis? Why do you include both Amanda and Lucy on your shortlist but not me or even Rory?"

"Too thick," Cade said.

"A fair call."

"Actually it was me who ruled you out," Jayne said. "Because you seemed so genuinely upset over Cade's accident."

"What does Francis's accident have to do with anything?"

Jayne tried to keep her face impassive but she was unsuccessful.

"No more secrets," Aubrey said. "Whatever else you're holding back, bring it out."

"Very well then," Jayne said. "Brace yourself Cade. This happened on the day of Caroline's memorial, shortly before we went to the ceremony. John Lambert pulled me to one side, and said that word had got round that you were 'meddling'. That's how he described it, it's not my phrase. Then he told me to warn you off any further investigations as 'lives were at risk'. I was reluctant to tell you until you were feeling stronger."

"Good god. You can star him doubly and trebly," Aubrey said. "Never liked the fellow. Cold."

"Did John suggest that someone ran me over deliberately?" Cade asked. He did look whiter than before, and Jayne felt a rush of guilt. She should never have said anything.

"Actually no. Or rather he didn't say either way. From what I could work out he was suggesting such a thing might be a possibility if you continued your investigations."

There was an uneasy silence.

"So where do we go from here?" Jayne asked.

"Whitehall," Aubrey replied. His joviality had gone, replaced by a sense of purpose. "By way of Amanda.

We'll need to bring her into our confidence of course, despite your suspicions."

"Ours? You don't suspect as well that she may be the second recruit?"

"No. It's far more likely to be one of the other three, in my view. Even you or Francis, on face value, though given the circumstances clearly not. I won't waste time on an elaborate web of bluff and double bluff. But even if so, if I am mistaken about Amanda, it's still a risk we need to take. We need someone with inside access to the government, and if it is her, well, I'm sure that will become apparent through the process of asking."

"Amanda's department isn't exactly in the inner sanctum of state secrets," Jayne said.

"She may have to put her thinking cap on, but she's several steps ahead of us in terms of access," Aubrey said. "If there are files to find, or even people to slip the wink, she's at least inside the building."

Cade hadn't said anything for a while, since Jayne's revelations. Now he spoke.

"I'm not sure we're taking the right approach. I don't mean to suggest that Lambert's message has in any way intimidated me. But everything so far is hunches and suppositions and rumours. I feel that we need facts. Dates. It's a lack of facts that caused all the complications in the first place. I mean the mix-up. If Harry had just bothered to do that one thing right, actually view the body. That was the main formality he was needed for and he flunked it," Cade said. He sounded strangely angry.

"Don't be too hard on him," Jayne said. "He was in shock, in a foreign country. A lot of people are very squeamish about death. And he had no reason to think that there were multiple casualties, or that identification was in any way in doubt. He obviously feels truly terrible about it now, and he partly blames himself for her death."

"Does he? Anyway, seeing how I'm out of action for a while, on the doctors' insistence, I shall spend my convalescence by collecting the facts and figures that we have been so casual about thus far. A simple call to Lucy's office, for example, would establish whether she was overseas around the time of Caroline's death."

"Many of us do travel frequently for both work and pleasure," Aubrey said. "You can hardly commandeer all of our passports and travel itineraries with a wave of your hand from the sickbed."

"I must do what I can," Cade said.

22

Amanda lived in Shepherd's Bush, renting a basement flat from a couple who worked at the BBC. On weekends she often went to visit her parents in Surrey, but by good fortune she was still in London when Jayne rang. Jayne explained that she was at a bit of a loose end now Cade was home, and would Amanda like to go for lunch?

Amanda invited her round instead, so Jayne caught a train and walked until she came to a tall, narrow house that matched the address. She was surprised how light and pleasant the flat was, so often basements were dark and dank. But the back of the flat was almost ground level, with doors opening onto a sort of sunken courtyard, private from the rest of the garden above that joined directly with the house. Some tubs of geraniums added colour, and there was a small patio table and chairs.

"It's quite a good sun-trap, and well sheltered," Amanda said, as she led Jayne there. "But let me know if you aren't warm enough, and we can go inside."

Jayne was very happy to sit outside, and said so. She had brought a bottle of wine and a flan, which Amanda took into the kitchen.

"It's a huge relief about Cade," Amanda said. "Almost a miracle that he escaped worse injury."

"He has no memory of how it happened, but he can fortunately recall everything leading up to it, at least up to the time he left his flat."

Was it her imagination or did Amanda look slightly disconcerted?

"So you'll be heading home soon, I expect?" she asked Jayne.

"That's the plan eventually, but for now, there's something of a situation that we want to resolve."

"We being the royal We? Or there are others involved?"

"Cade and Aubrey. And that's partly why I'm here. You as well, if you're willing."

Amanda smiled wryly. "Nothing surprises me with Cade, his life is a melodrama. And Aubrey's would be too, at least if he allowed any drama to happen to him rather than watching everyone else's through binoculars. Anyway, go on."

"It's not actually about Cade or Aubrey. It's about Caroline." And Jayne filled Amanda in, including the conversation with John.

"It's like a game of Murder in the Dark," Amanda said. "Eight of us - no, seven of course now - running around and wondering which of us is secretly a spy. Except of course it's not a game, is it, because Caroline is dead?"

"Everything seemed rather unreal, until Cade was hit."

"And you think that may have been deliberate. I must say, John's warning is strange. Not so much what he said, but how he said it. To you, I mean. Cade was in hospital at that point, so it was hardly urgent. Though maybe that's why, because I believe John is overseas again at the moment, so didn't know when he might be able to speak with Cade himself. Or perhaps he thought Cade would pay it more heed, coming from you?"

"I wondered about that. I delayed telling him, but we've reached the point where we just need everything on the table," Jayne said. "The problem is that John's warning presented the possibility that Cade's accident was not an accident. Thinking that someone tried to take you out, and only narrowly missed, is not pleasant."

"So in the very worst case scenario, one of us is not only an agent, but a defector and a murderer?" Amanda said.

It was the first time it had been said so clearly and starkly. It sounded shrill and absurd, yet with the sinking, heavy feeling beneath that this was so, and there was no way back.

"My first thought, and hear me out, for it's not necessarily my preferred course of action, is whether we should even attempt to do anything," Amanda said. "The damage is done and we cannot bring Caroline back. Rumours must have reached the right ears about this suspected double dealing in Greece, and official wheels must surely have been set in motion. If it is the case, it will eventually be exposed. And even if not publicly so - in terms of newspapers, I mean - we should still certainly be aware of the outcome."

"Not taking action would also avoid future harm to any of us," Jayne said.

"And yet, you feel as I do, that it just isn't right to do nothing. We cannot simply let it lie. My second thought, then, is to contact the authorities, but I see obvious obstacles there. For starters we have no official murder. Caroline's death was certified as an accident, possibly suicide from what Harry told you, though I imagine he has kept such reports away from his family if they do include those details. They would be written in Greek anyway. Jurisdiction is a significant issue, since the death was in Greece. Then there are the practicalities of what such an investigation would involve."

"Caroline's family have been very much in my mind," Jayne said. "To reopen their grief, when as you say, it won't bring her back, is not something to be considered lightly."

"Would they take comfort from knowing their daughter died in service to her country, rather than by accident? Or would it be an extra source of pain, knowing there was an intention and a cause? How does it make us feel?" Amanda asked.

"At first, I was shocked and bewildered at her death. And very sad. But in the process of remembering her, I've felt more angry at the loss. She was a kind and good person, a worthwhile person. Her cousin Lucas mentioned that she planned to turn part of the family house into a convalescent home."

"They've certainly got room for that," Amanda said. "I wonder what will happen to it now. It's down to Harry now, at least when he inherits. They'll have to do something with it sooner or later, it haemorrhages money, like so many of these old places. Unusually it's not entailed on a male heir, which I believe helps the tax situation."

"It's so beautiful though, it must be very hard to have to change it," Jayne said.

She thought back to the house, imagining it a couple of centuries ago, thronging with people: extended family, staff, guests. The grounds at the peak of their beauty with a multitude of gardeners. She had even seen a painting of it in early Victorian times, showing a garden party with guests rather fancifully dressed, sailing in swan-shaped boats on the lake. Jayne wondered what had happened to them, and if they had really existed beyond the artist's imagination.

And now just two people lived there, growing older, one of their children dead and the other living elsewhere. Its glory days as a family home were long past.

Amanda continued. "Finally, then, my third thought, is to carry out some discreet inquiries, and decide what to do with any discovery if and when we make it. Which I am sure is where you, Cade and Aubrey think I can help." Amanda poured them both some more wine.

"We're aware it might not be easy, or even possible, but Aubrey felt that your position gives you at least some advantage."

"What makes it difficult is that I don't really know what I'm looking for," Amanda said. "I have no idea what kind of files may be kept, nor where. I suspect that at most I shall only be able to access very low level material that may not give us any answers."

She looked directly at Jayne. "And then of course you have to face the possibility that it could be me."

"Actually you were in fact Cade's top pick, along with John and Lucy. Aubrey was most put out not to make the shortlist."

Amanda laughed. "Aubrey is the last person one would pick, isn't he? And yet perhaps that's why he'd be the first person. He travels frequently too. However if I looked at it dispassionately, based solely on each of our circumstances, I have to say I'd pick you."

"My circumstances are exceedingly quiet and dull," Jayne said.

"You have no ties. You are at leisure. No one keeps a check on your movements, such as an employer, or a roommate. You are highly intelligent and resourceful. And you were in Greece during all the time everything happened."

"I can only tell you that it isn't me."

"Likewise," Amanda said. "And I think that's another very good reason why we do need to do something. Because right now, we are all living under this terrible suspicion of one another. Aubrey, Cade, you and I, and Lucy's no fool, she'll eventually find out. John presumably already has an inkling. Even Rory isn't that thick-skinned."

"You mentioned John was overseas again. Is he abroad frequently?"

"I don't really keep across his movements. At the funeral he mentioned something about being on the continent earlier in the month, so I was surprised to hear he was overseas again, since his work is here."

"If an agent has defected or become a double agent, or whatever the correct terminology is, and word is out, wouldn't they go into hiding, or across enemy lines?" Jayne asked.

"I suspect the relevant authorities don't know who it is yet either," Amanda said. "They presumably have a report, even evidence, of collaboration, but they may not know which individual operative is involved. There would be more than just Caroline and Person X in the field."

"So there's no real certainty, or even reason to suspect, that the second agent from our set - Person X - is the one in question?"

"None at all, when you put it like that. But you think it is, don't you? It's a feeling - there's a wrong'un in our midst. And Cade meeting with a nasty accident certainly brings it closer to home."

23

Lucas had invited Jayne to dinner and insisted on picking her up from Aubrey's. He was more good looking than ever in a flawlessly tailored suit that matched his dark grey eyes. Jayne felt a secret, illicit delight to be in his company and wondered if he had told Victoria that he was meeting her.

Aubrey, who had plans of his own to attend an auction that evening, offered Lucas a drink. But an early reservation had been made, so Lucas and Jayne had to leave straight away and hail a taxi.

As Jayne picked up the wrap she had intended to wear, Aubrey thrust a different one at her. It was a more showy piece of fabric than the plain black one she had chosen, in a dark amber colour with fine beadwork. "Brings out your eyes," he said under his breath. Jayne took it, telling herself she was only doing so to please Aubrey.

"The restaurant is in Seven Dials so we could have walked," Lucas said, "but unfortunately I got held up on some business." He had been twenty minutes late, and was sincerely apologetic.

Jayne had given some considerable thought as to how much she should tell Lucas. In the end she had decided to hold nothing back. Even Harry's accusation that Lucas had caused Caroline's heartbreak. No one believed the suicide story anyway. But she still found herself curious. It was part of the puzzle of Caroline: had she really spent her years pining away for her older cousin?

Knowing and regretting the years wasted on her own futile heartache for Rory, Jayne hoped not.

Fortunately there were plenty of cabs about and it was only a short drive, so they arrived in good time. If the night stayed mild, Jayne thought that it would be nice to walk back later on.

The restaurant was the kind of place that Jayne would have never found by herself. It wasn't ostentatiously fashionable nor expensive yet she had the sense that it would be very difficult for just anyone to get a table. Other diners there were elegantly, even expensively dressed, yet it was all very discreet. Though she did not recognise anyone, she felt that there were powerful people here, even famous people. A few of them certainly looked familiar.

As if reading her mind, Lucas said: "They can be frustratingly capricious about reservations here, though I haven't personally had trouble."

Less capricious and more discerning, Jayne thought. She could see why they would happily grant Lucas a table, but she suspected that some of Cade's more exuberant theatrical associates might be politely refused.

"The food's not too bad, but the best thing is that it's quiet enough to talk. Let's order first, because there's a lot to tell."

The menu was entirely in French, with no English translation. Jayne managed to make her way through most of it, her A-level French not as rusty as she feared. It was a good menu, featuring traditional French cuisine but with some interesting choices. Jayne recognised *perdreau*, and having always wanted to try partridge, chose that.

"I am sorry I didn't manage to speak to you at Caroline's memorial," Lucas said. "It was all very rushed, and my aunt and uncle needed my assistance with certain matters."

Jayne felt some guilt since she had deliberately avoided getting into a conversation with him, but relief that he apparently hadn't realised.

"I must apologise as well for being so unavailable," she said. "We were all quite frantic about Cade. His mother has been staying here, she's from the North East, and it has been a very stressful time for her."

"I was very relieved to hear that he recovered so well," Lucas said.

"He was very lucky, as it turned out. Almost a miracle that he wasn't more badly hurt. Now I also have a lot to tell you, and I admit that I have delayed part of it, but I hope you will understand why when I explain," Jayne said.

"Which of us should go first? Why don't you start, as you have already been waiting some time to do so."

Jayne twisted the hem of her napkin in her lap. "Very well. Just after Cade's accident, I bumped into Harry. He revealed to me a very bizarre story that goes some way to explain, at least, why I did in fact see Caroline several days after she was originally thought to be dead." She explained to Lucas about the suicide attempt claim and the subsequent mix up in the hospital.

"I confess that I did at first accept everything Harry said at face value, but that was partly out of my own shock and confusion," Jayne said. "In no way do I now think, even for a moment, that Caroline would have done something like that, let alone twice. It simply wasn't in her character. It's clear that someone has pulled the wool over Harry's eyes, and likely the Greek police's eyes too, which I believe is supported by the other information I have to pass on."

She told him about Cade's and Aubrey's respective discoveries.

"That there were two agents recruited from our year is coincidence enough," Jayne continued. "That the second agent should also not only have been in Greece, but also be some kind of defector or double agent, would seem a stretch too far. And yet we all feel a kind of chill." She paused for a moment, and Lucas did not interrupt her. "I think because there is something personal about this. The suggestion of suicide, it suggests personal knowledge of Caroline, even if they grossly misjudged her nature."

"What do you mean by personal knowledge?" Lucas asked.

"The fact that it was attributed to unhappiness over her love life. I'm not sure how Harry came to that information, I should have asked. Perhaps there was a forged suicide note. The more I think of it, the odder it is, unless Harry had previous suspicions."

"What exactly was said?"

Jayne bit her lip. This was the one part she had desperately hoped to avoid mentioning. "This is terribly awkward, but I suppose it may explain some of the tension that you mentioned between you and Harry. You see, Harry believed that Caroline was depressed because of having unrequited love for you."

Lucas was incredulous. "How absolutely absurd! Harry should have known better, surely!"

"Caroline was very fond of you, she talked about you at university, as I think I've mentioned," Jayne said, in explanation. "That's why it didn't seem so far-fetched when Harry first suggested it. I don't suppose that she did perhaps have feelings that you weren't aware of, but Harry was?" She hated asking, but they needed everything out in the open.

"Let me tell you about Caroline and me," Lucas said. "We grew up very close together for most of our childhood: Caroline, Harry and I, and our other cousins. Mainly because of the house; while our grandparents lived there, it was the ideal place to spend school holidays. Caroline and I were particularly close. She was like a little sister to me, I have no other siblings. Harry was younger, and not always the easiest of boys. As we grew up, she would confide in me and I in her." He paused while a waiter refilled their glasses.

"I can tell you that she spent most of her teenage years pining for the family groom, not for me. That was her serious heartache. We also used to discuss her hopes and plans for the house, and her fears of how her parents would cope with the increasing cost and tax burden as they grew older. She knew the house would be hers someday, and she wanted to be more prepared than they were."

"It's unusual that it would pass to Caroline, isn't it? Amanda mentioned something about entails," Jayne said.

"Yes. Actually it is entailed, only not on the male heir, but the first born. A rather more equitable situation though as you say, unusual."

I doubt Harry felt that way, thought Jayne. It must have rankled, losing out to a sister.

"So you are absolutely certain that she wasn't carrying a torch for you that Harry became aware of?"

"Jayne, the groom was female."

This was a startling revelation. But looking back, Jayne realised that it made sense why it was so easy for Harry and for her to have supposed that Lucas was the object of Caroline's affection. Since she never talked about or showed interest in any other men, but had a well-known, high regard for her cousin, it was all too easy to have added two and two and made five.

"Now I feel very foolish," Jayne said.

"Don't be. Whatever it was, it didn't define her. It may only have been a teenage thing. Caroline didn't give herself much of a chance after she left school in terms of having a personal life. I did worry about it, but the house seemed to be her main passion. I suspect that had she married, or found herself a life partner, it would have happened later on."

"She was happy at university," Jayne said. "If you've ever worried about that, please don't. We roomed together in the second year, and Caroline led a very full and sociable life. We didn't share intimate confidences, but I'm certain she enjoyed her time there."

They had finished their meal, and Lucas suggested going on to a club for coffee. "We can continue our conversation there. You'll like the club, I think."

If the restaurant was selective, the club seemed absolutely exclusive. It was to all intents and purposes hidden away, just an unmarked door in the street. That door led into a plainly painted corridor, until they turned a corner and reached another, interior door, painted dark green. Here a man stood, who nodded to Lucas, but did not ask for any identification. Either he recognised Lucas, or Lucas simply passed muster.

On entering, Jayne half expected to find herself in some kind of illegal opium den. Instead, it was more like a private, elegant party, and also like stepping out of London into another world. A woman sang softly in French on a small stage at one end of the room, accompanied by a couple of musicians. Floor length windows along one wall opened onto a balcony.

"I think the night is mild enough to sit outside, if you're not too cold," Lucas said.

The balcony looked over gardens at the back of other houses, a generous green space hidden from the street. Jasmine climbed up the wall below, spilling over the top. "How incredible that this is here, tucked away like this," Jayne said.

A waiter came up to take their orders, and when he had gone Lucas turned to her. "Now it's my turn. It's far less astounding a revelation than yours, but possibly significant."

"Go on."

"Maria Tsakalotos. One of ours apparently. Not the simple Greek girl we had imagined."

"One of ours - you mean another agent? For Britain?"

"Exactly so."

"So that means two agents, killed within a week," Jayne said. "Clearly the deaths are linked."

She was thinking furiously. How did this all fit in with Harry's account? "So Maria is killed, and Caroline injured. Caroline manages to get out of hospital. Then a few days later someone - the second agent - gets her."

"We still can't be sure of that," Lucas said.

"But it must have been the same person who killed both of them?"

"If they were killed for the same reason, then yes. I think the priority now is tracing this mysterious boyfriend, the 'Englishman'."

"You think he's the one?" That would narrow it to John or Rory. Or Aubrey, she supposed. Cade had a clear alibi, he would have been on stage every night that week. Unless his understudy had filled in. How quickly could one get to Athens and back? She briefly imagined Amanda with a fake beard but dismissed the vision almost instantly.

Lucas stood up. "Let's dance," he said.

"Dance?" Jayne was taken aback.

"It might clear our heads."

Jayne highly doubted that closer proximity to Lucas would clear her head, but she allowed him to lead her back into the room where several couples were already moving together on the floor. It was rather like something out of an old film, she thought. It wasn't the first time she had danced with Lucas, though on the previous occasion it had not been intentional.

Jayne remembered how she was thrown against him by the crowd, in the torchlit darkness amid the ruins. That was spontaneous, a dance by accident. The music was wild, and the atmosphere unearthly. This was a conscious choice yet with the same strange sense of unreality. For the first time that night she gave some thought to Victoria. Did Lucas bring her here as well? Would he tell her they had dined together?

Being in his arms again was wonderful, even though she reminded herself it meant nothing. It was just a social thing. But this time Lucas was holding himself nearer her, with no pressure from the crowd. When they started dancing the music had been slow, stately. As the dancing progressed it accelerated, to a gypsy jazz, the whirling rhythm and pace transporting her back to the frenzy of the Greek folk musicians and their lightning violins.

They were laughing as they tried to keep up, to catch their breath. When the music finally stopped, Lucas held on to her and she looked up at him, her eyes shining as he gazed at her. For a moment the room seemed empty, there was silence. Then it all slid back, the people, the ambience, and the musicians picked up their instruments and began another tune.

PART THREE

Betrayal

24

It was in the dead of night that it came to Jayne. Something so obvious, so inconsistent that she was amazed that none of them had picked it up before.

She had insisted they walk back from the club. Lucas suggested a taxi, but Jayne felt reckless, free, she wanted to enjoy and extend the night. He had his arm around her as they walked back through Seven Dials towards Bloomsbury. Everything had changed, and she embraced it.

He had dropped her off at Aubrey's flat, wanting to see her safely inside, but Jayne hadn't wanted to disturb Aubrey. So he kissed her for the first time on the doorstep, and she went upstairs elated, to find Aubrey still up, enjoying a nightcap.

"My choice of stole was in order," he said, smug with the satisfaction of the successful Cupid. Jayne didn't even try to protest. She felt so utterly changed inside that her hair may as well have been strewn with roses, her clothes decked with gold.

Still dancing inside, she declined a nightcap and went off to bed, falling asleep almost instantly. But instead of lovely dreams inspired by the evening, she saw dark shapes and drowned faces. Caroline was there, trying to tell her something, all sound lost in the water that covered her.

It was a horrible dream, of shadows and death, snuffing out the euphoria she had gone to bed with. Beyond Caroline's face, more distant, and yet still calling out to her, was Maria Tsakalotos. "Where am I?" she cried, and Jayne woke with a start, to a feeling of strange loneliness and terror.

Where was Maria? Why were there posters of her, why was she still missing if Harry had told her the truth and the mix-up had been corrected? If they had repatriated Caroline's body, as he claimed, Maria would surely have been quickly identified as the earlier body and her relatives duly informed.

For the first time, Jayne tried discounting everything Harry had told her. She had already dismissed parts of it, attributing to error on his part, or his being deliberately misled. Caroline's suicide attempt, for example. Where did it leave them if every part was untrue, even a lie?

For now she didn't want to consider the implications of the untruth, it was too much to take in. She held that awareness at arm's length, and went through the facts as though it was a puzzle.

Really it was quite simple. What were the things she had been told by Harry, and only Harry? How did it all fit together if she went solely by what she had learned out there, what the police and townsfolk had told her? And how far back should she take it? Harry claimed to have been summoned by the police because Caroline was dead, but was even that true? Might he have gone there earlier?

Jayne had written down some notes one night, trying to get her head around the dates, and now she took them out and looked over them again.

Maria had gone missing the night after Hekatombaion, at the end of June. The next day, a body had been found off an island called Nisis Lathrémporos, according to Jayne's notes. The police considered it to be Caroline, and Harry had formally identified it as such couple of days later.

One week later, Jayne had seen Caroline, alive and well.

Some time, within the first two weeks of July, a body had been flown back, and buried as Caroline.

Those were the facts. The police had never mentioned a second death, nor had anyone in the town. A second woman found dead would have instantly raised speculation that it was Maria. But there was no second body, and no speculation.

And no one had heard from Caroline since.

Jayne shivered in her bed. The curtains were heavy, of a thick, expensive material, but there was a thin gap at one side that allowed sickly yellow streetlight to seep through. It was better than total darkness.

It was time to confront Harry's role. What if he had deliberately identified the body of another woman in place of his sister, knowing full well that Caroline was alive? On the face of it this seemed pointless, he would have been rapidly found out once Caroline resurfaced. But she did not resurface. Harry must have known that she would not.

But why? As she thought about the blustering, petulant young man, with his schoolboy face and resentment, snatches of conversation came back to her. *"She knew the house would be hers someday." "It's down to Harry now, at least when he inherits."*

Might this not be about espionage and intrigue after all? Could Harry have wanted Caroline dead to inherit in her place? Other words drifted back to her. *"People only ever really kill for money."* John's observation, but who had repeated it, was it Aubrey? Cade?

And what had happened to Caroline? Had Harry told his lies to the police, informed his devastated parents, and then lain in wait to kill his sister? Where was her body?

Still none of it made any sense; there were more questions than answers. What was the point of two deaths? Could Harry have also killed Maria, and then planted some possession of Caroline's on her, to aid the misidentification? Was he the mysterious "Englishman" that had been seen with her in the months before her death?

First and foremost, she needed to establish when Harry had actually flown out to Greece. Cade was right, they had been very careless about dates and alibis. Until now though she hadn't even considered Harry being involved. Harry's story was that he had been called by the police, and then flown over, after the first of July.

Jayne longed for it not to be three o'clock in the early hours of the morning, to instead have Cade and Aubrey there and their wise counsel. And Lucas.

She feared she would lie there until dawn, the horror and the questions swirling around her mind. Instead she fell into a deeper sleep, unaware as the streetlamp faded, replaced by a thin line of dawn light.

Jayne knew something was wrong when Aubrey came into her room to wake her. Usually she was up first, and in the rare instances she wasn't, he never did more than knock on the door. He couldn't bear alarm clocks, so there wasn't even one in the spare room.

"Jayne, are you awake? I'm afraid there's been some bad news."

Her first thought was that it was Cade, and the despair was a lead weight inside her, making her want to keep her eyes closed, sink down into the mattress, and only wake again for it not to be true.

"It's Amanda. I'm afraid she's dead."

Guilt hung over her, a black shroud of despair. She had bidden Amanda "meddle" despite what had happened to Cade, and despite the warning that John had given her. Were it not for her request, Amanda might be safely home in her lovely flat right now, having breakfast as usual, getting ready for work.

There was no doubt about it being deliberate. Someone had struck Amanda with a blunt object as she left her office the previous evening. There were no signs of a robbery or any subsequent assault, and nothing to suggest an accident or any other motive.

It would make the newspapers of course, with Amanda's Whitehall job only adding to the headlines. Jayne thought of Major and Mrs Charles, down in Surrey. There was a younger sister too, still at school.

"This is not about blame," Aubrey told her, putting food before her and insisting that she eat something. "This is about how critically important it is that Caroline's and Amanda's murderer is brought to justice. It underlines the necessity of what we have been trying to do, even if we have erred in the method, with these tragic consequences."

Jayne wished she had his single mindedness. How could she not blame herself? They knew what had happened to Cade, and they had put Amanda at obvious risk.

"I think I know who killed her," Jayne said. "And Caroline too." And she told Aubrey about her revelations in the middle of the night.

He was silent for a while, and Jayne could tell how intently he was going over it in his mind, with a slight frown on his brow.

"That's certainly a very different theory from what we have been basing our investigations on. It can't be dismissed, certainly. Not until we know more facts: Harry's whereabouts last night, most specifically."

Margaret Cade had only just gone back home, and Jayne was worried about the impact that learning of Amanda's death might have on Cade. He still seemed fragile, there were circles under his eyes and he had lost weight since his accident.

"He needs to be out treading the boards, not pining away in here," Aubrey said.

They had gone round to his flat to tell him in person.

"It's Amanda isn't it?" he had said when he opened the door and saw them. "Tell me the worst."

"She was attacked; she didn't make it." Blunt, but what else to say?

"I knew something like this would happen," Cade said as he ushered them in, his new dressing gown trailing from his angular frame. He looked lost. "I should shower and dress. And then I have absolutely no idea what we should do."

He left them and went to shower. Jayne had never seen him like this before. The accident had taken far more out of him than she had realised. And this latest shock might be enough to put him over the edge.

"It's how he copes," Aubrey said. "He's like this before a first night."

Jayne wasn't sure. She remembered Cade's first night nerves from university productions. He was brittle, but still flippant. Now he seemed broken.

She went into the kitchen to make some coffee. Thanks to Mrs Cade's recent residence it was well stocked with fresh milk and clean cups. She also put some toast on.

While they waited for Cade there was a knock at the door. It was Lucy. "I heard on the radio earlier this morning," she said. "They didn't give out her name, but somehow just from the details I had an awful feeling. So I tried to ring her but there was no reply. And then I rang Aubrey, and when there was no reply there as well, I knew."

She was very white, but held onto her self-possession. "I couldn't think what else to do, or where else you would all be except here. How on earth could something like this happen? Why on earth would someone attack Amanda?"

Jayne had forgotten that Lucy didn't really know anything about their investigation. Now was certainly not the time to bring her up to date. She gave Aubrey a glance, and he indicated that he understood.

Then Cade emerged. He was wearing black, which was quite usual for him, but now seemed like mourning.

"Her parents will know by now," Aubrey said.

"I have a spare key to her flat. I'm not sure if her parents do," Lucy said.

"Let's establish where they've taken her," Aubrey said. "You and I will go there, Lucy, as you were best acquainted with the family. We shall give them the keys, and offer our assistance in any way we can."

Jayne appreciated Aubrey taking control. He was really no older than them, but today his avuncular role took on a new strength. He did not state that she should stay there to look after Cade, but she took it as understood. Getting Lucy away from Cade, who might let something slip, was also wise.

Aubrey made a couple of phone calls; while he did so they sat around in silence. Cade nursed the coffee Jayne had made him but did not drink it.

After Aubrey and Lucy left, Jayne sat nearer Cade and took his hand.

"It will be alright," she said. "Not for some time perhaps, but this will end. It will be over."

"I thought it would get better once I came home. My mother did her best, and I managed to fob her off as far as possible or she would have never gone home, but it gets worse each day. And now this."

"Perhaps you could go and stay with her?"

Cade shook his head. "It wouldn't make any difference. There's work to consider as well. I have to get back out, somehow."

"Your mother spoke to me quite a bit about you while you were unconscious," Jayne said. "You haven't told her, have you? She mentioned grandchildren."

"It's not impossible. I might adopt someday. Or try something lavender."

"That's surely not necessary, in this day and age?" Jayne asked.

"You never know. Certain roles get shut off when it's widely known. Even if you pretend to flit a bit both ways it's easier." He touched Jayne's hair, drawing out a strand. "I should marry you. At least you'd be reasonably decorative and half decent at cooking."

Jayne smiled. "Do you know, there was a time once when I think I might have even accepted you. But that was when I couldn't imagine anything else, that anything would change."

"You mean Rory? And now it's all different. You're all different. I've blown my chance." A fragment of the wry humour flickered anew, but his eyes remained sad.

"You're the third person to say that. I don't know why, nothing has changed for me."

"Yes it has," Cade said. "You were beautiful before, now you are radiant. A veil is lifted. Even today, after this. But surely it's not Rory?"

"No, it's not." Such irony that it finally could be, if she wanted it to, after all this time.

"It's the cousin then."

Jayne said nothing. The elation of last night, followed by the horror of today, was unthinkable. How would Lucas find out? she wondered. From the news, or would someone call him? Should she call him?

As so often happened, Cade read her mind. "I'll get Aubrey to ring him. I should do it myself, but it's no good. I couldn't say the words."

"No one would expect you to."

"What are you going to do about the fiancée?" Cade said. "I suppose it's mutual with you and him? Will he break it off with her?"

"It hasn't been mentioned. Everything happened so unexpectedly. I'm not at all sure of what will happen."

Cade looked at her, studying her. 'What's your biggest fear, Jayne?"

She was silent for a moment, lost in thought, though she already knew the answer. "Going home again, back to how it was before. Forgetting all over again."

25

There they were again, the three of them, sitting around Cade's flat. Lucy had stayed with Amanda's family. Jayne took the opportunity to remind Cade that Lucy knew nothing, and that he should be as circumspect as possible around her.

"It's already complicated enough. We don't need to drag anyone else into it," she said.

"We'll have to talk to the police at some point," Aubrey said. "The question is, what do we three tell them?"

"What do we really know?" Cade replied.

It had seemed like a game before, a puzzle. Now it was a mess of suspicion, confused ideas and distrust, at least in Jayne's perception.

"How on earth do we link all this to Caroline, and to the attack on Cade?" she said. "Would they even take us seriously? Would they arrest Harry?"

"Harry?" said Cade, sharply. "Why on earth would they arrest Harry?"

Jayne realised she hadn't even told him about her recent thoughts. She gave him a brief summary of the inconsistencies she had noted the night before.

"Just because he lied, doesn't mean he did it," Cade said. "Besides..."

"Besides what?" Jayne asked.

"He couldn't have. Let me show you my list." He brought out some pieces of paper, scrawled over in biro with various names, dates and other comments. "I finally put down on paper who could have been there for the two deaths. In Greece, I haven't had a chance to consider last night, of course."

They looked at Cade's piece of paper. The main item on it was a list of names - their names - with two columns next to them. The first was titled "1st" and the second was titled "7th". "We don't know exactly when Caroline died," Cade said, "but we do know that she wasn't seen after that day."

Jayne saw that there was a cross in both columns next to her name. "Does this mean I'm off the hook?" she asked.

"Quite the opposite. X marks the spot. You were there during both dates. I didn't have access to people's passport stamps and ticket stubs, so this was the best I could do."

They looked down the list, with Cade providing commentary. "I wasn't away, of course, the theatre will vouch for that. I even did the matinée that week because my understudy had a sore throat. You were overseas, Aubrey, over both dates."

"I haven't denied it. I was on one of my antiques hunts."

"Lucy was also away, though only for the first date," Cade continued. "She was back soon after, because she heard about Caroline from Harry before he flew out. That's how I found out, and I told Aubrey. Anyway, Amanda was in London over both dates. John is the only one I haven't been able to ascertain. And Rory was overseas, but then he's always overseas," he said. "He's off again now, even though he was supposed to be staying in London until the New Year."

Jayne felt a sense of relief at this. Then she remembered what Amanda had said. "John may have been overseas too. Amanda said something about him being on the continent, though she didn't say where," Jayne said.

"And then his warning," Cade said. He looked at Aubrey.

"Except if you put a third column, Cade, titled Last Night, you'll unfortunately have to put a cross for John. Because he's apparently abroad again. We need two crosses and a blank, to qualify. We could also put a column for your accident, if that further narrows it down. The problem is that we don't know for absolutely certain whether it was intentional or not, so let's not include it for now."

"That leaves you then, and Aubrey."

"We're also one another's alibis for last night. Though I suppose one of us could have sneaked out later on. When was the attack on Amanda supposed to have happened?"

"Late evening, around nine o'clock," Aubrey said. "When you were at dinner with Lucas."

"That rules me out then. Given it's obviously not Aubrey, what about Harry?"

"I told you he couldn't have done it," Cade said, "besides which he's not one of us. Why the fixation with him? He can't be the second agent, there's no motive."

"The house. With Caroline dead, it's his. The entail meant that she got everything before, he would have been penniless. Now it's all his, or will be when his parents die," Jayne explained.

Aubrey got up and went and wound Cade's clock that sat on the mantelpiece and had long stopped ticking. It was a fine object, elegantly carved, likely a gift from him to Cade.

"I tell you that he couldn't have done it. He wasn't in Greece for the first."

"How can you be certain?" Jayne asked.

"Lucy spoke with him. As I said, he told her about Caroline."

"Did Lucy actually see him though, or did he call her? He could have easily done so from Greece, and pretended he was about to leave."

"Just take my word for it, he was not in Greece on the first," Cade said.

Without meaning to, they were somehow arguing. It must be the stress. Cade was looking sullen and also, Jayne was intrigued to see, slightly embarrassed. Aubrey was still fiddling with the clock, apparently paying them no attention.

"We can't just take anyone's word for anything, at a time like this," she persisted.

There was silence. Suddenly Cade burst out, with an edge of bitterness in his voice:

"Harry wasn't there on the first because Harry was here with me."

173

There was an even lengthier silence at this revelation, then Cade continued miserably.

"It's not something I'm proud of. It was only an occasional thing. Boredom, or loneliness on my part. Right after that occasion, on the first of July, he went to Greece. So I know he couldn't have been there the night of the festival with the unmanageable name, when the first girl was killed, because he was right here in this flat, with me.

"And last night, when Amanda was killed, he was here with me again."

They were at an impasse. Down to zero suspects. Either they had been barking up completely the wrong tree, or at least one of the deaths was simply a tragic accident.

Aubrey suggested they all dine with him that evening, rather than stay alone. It was partly to get Cade out of his flat as he hadn't been outside since his return from hospital. "Take a taxi," Aubrey advised him. "Don't bother walking to the tube if it brings on the shell shock. It's to be expected at this stage."

Jayne was going to go back and help prepare, while Aubrey went for groceries, but she could tell that Cade was nervous about being left alone.

"Why don't you come with me now, there's no sense us travelling separately. I'd be glad of the company," she said.

This was a lie, as she longed for some time alone. She had so many things churning around in her head, and really wanted some peace and quiet to sit down and assess her thoughts on everything. But Cade was very vulnerable right now, and he took priority.

As she had expected, Cade agreed and they went outside to get a taxi together. Cade was clearly struggling beyond the confines of his flat. Cars driving past were terrifying him, and Jayne saw him flinch at particularly fast or loud vehicles. Even though he seemed calmer once inside the taxi, it was a relief to finally reach Bloomsbury and get him into Aubrey's flat.

"I doubt there's anything much to do. His Mrs H is so efficient that there's not so much as a speck of tarnish to polish off a butter knife," Cade said. There was a vestige of his old flippancy, but he still looked haunted.

"If you're busy with things I might read," he said.

There was nothing for Jayne to be busy with, but this gave her the chance to be alone for a moment. She went into the bedroom she was staying in, and lay down on the bed. She was about to close her eyes when she suddenly realised how exhausted she was, and that if she let herself sleep, she would be out for hours. She would have to keep busy somehow.

Painfully, she got up again, and tried to find some activity to stay up for. A button needed sewing on one of her blouses, but that would take all of five minutes. Reading might be the best way to calm her thoughts, and then she could let her mind wander even as her hands turned the pages. She went to join Cade in the library end of Aubrey's sitting room, when the telephone rang.

It was Lucas. He had heard about Amanda.

"Terrible news like this travels quickly. I wanted to ring you anyway, to thank you for last night."

Jayne returned her thanks. She was relieved that he had managed to find out. It spared her having to tell him over the phone.

"Would you like me to come over?" he asked.

This was a dilemma. On one hand Jayne would have loved to see him. On the other hand she was anxious about Cade, and thought there was a chance he might open up to her if they were there alone.

"It's very kind of you but Cade is here, and Aubrey will be back soon."

"I'll call you tomorrow then. Please pass on my condolences to the others."

Jayne put the telephone handset back. Returning to her plan of reading, she went through some of the books on one of Aubrey's shelves.

As expected, many of them covered antiques and fine art, as well as Classical antiquities. Aubrey was fortunate to have private interests that overlapped so closely with his job. She picked up a volume on Hellenistic art and leafed through it.

Something fluttered from the pages onto the floor. Jayne picked it up, and saw a mixture of what appeared to be Greek and English lettering. She instantly recognised one word: HEKATOMBAION. With pictures of dancing silhouettes below, the paper was clearly a flyer for a Hekatombaion festival. Then she looked at the word above it.

Something Jayne had noticed during her time in Greece, mainly from studying menus, was how similar the capital letters were between the two alphabets. Many Greek letters were almost identical to the Roman alphabet, particularly in upper case. Or should it be the other way round, since Greek letters came first? It struck her the name HEKATOMBAION might equally be Greek or Roman, since by coincidence all of its ten different letters were identical in both writing systems.

But it was the word above that sent a chill through her. DELFINIAN. While certain letters were different, she had seen this word before, and it was instantly readable to her. Delphinian. This, then, was a piece of advertising for the Hekatombaion festival organised by the Delphinians, and thanks to Greek numerals she could instantly see the date. It was for this year.

How had the flyer come into Aubrey's possession? She herself was the obvious conduit, but she was certain she had never seen such a thing let alone brought it along with her in her luggage to Aubrey's. Even if she had, and even if she had left it lying around, Mrs H was so fastidious that any stray piece of paper would have immediately been placed neatly on Aubrey's desk, or on the chest of drawers in Jayne's room if her ownership was evident.

Besides which Jayne was certain she had never seen this flyer. Its similarity to other brochures and posters on the walls of the Delphinians' office had helped her recognise the word DELFINIANS, but she had never seen a poster for the Hekatombaion festival. She knew, because she and her cousins had actively looked for information about it, curious as to what the street party and procession were about. They had initially assumed it was some kind of saint's day.

"What's that?" Cade asked, looking up from his book.

"Just a leaflet left in one of Aubrey's art books."

Cade resumed his reading, but Jayne was very troubled. For Aubrey to have possession of this leaflet he must surely have been in Greece quite recently and in the same area, yet he had never mentioned anything about it. He often spoke at length about his purchasing trips overseas, but he had remained absolutely silent about this trip despite its obvious relevance.

Other than herself, Aubrey was the only person who could have been present for all three deaths. She thought back to the other night when she went out with Lucas. Good god, that was only last night. How much time seemed to have passed already.

So last night, after she had left, might Aubrey have also gone out? She tried to imagine kind, generous Aubrey creeping over to Whitehall with some kind of cosh and lying in wait for Amanda. It was an impossible vision. Yet the whole point of an agent was to lead a sort of double life so they must get used to dissembling. Was it possible, then, that both of Aubrey's personas were real? Her dear, amusing, clever friend from university, and some sort of ruthless, calculating operative, able to kill where necessary?

"Is anything wrong Jayne? You've done nothing but stare at that paper for fifteen minutes."

She made an excuse about dozing off, then put the leaflet back in the book and returned it to the shelf as she had found it. Taking another volume without even looking at the title, she sat in an armchair and returned to her thoughts, trying to turn the pages as though she was really reading.

Jayne desperately wanted to talk with Aubrey, alone. She had no idea how she could bring herself to level such an accusation against him. Was it even safe for her to do so? If he had killed Maria and Caroline and Amanda, would he shrink from adding her to the list? He had supported, even encouraged her investigations. Amanda's involvement had been his idea. Why then, if only to kill her? Was he worried that she might have taken it upon herself anyway, was it a kind of bluff?

Or was his concern all a front and instead, some bizarre psychotic motive had driven Aubrey to kill? He liked collecting antiquities, perhaps collecting victims was another hobby.

She felt wretched. Aubrey is one of my best, closest friends, she thought. How can I think this of him?

She needed someone to bring her back down to earth. To provide alternative reasons, to play devil's advocate, to find some extra snag that could absolve Aubrey.

"I'm sorry to intrude Jayne, but you seem very distracted," Cade interrupted her again. "And I don't feel much better myself. Let's have a drink." He went to Aubrey's cabinet and poured her a double brandy. "It's the best thing for stage fright. You look like you've seen a ghost," he said, looking more closely at her.

What could she say? What should she do? How could she even sit through a meal, with Aubrey, Cade and possibly Lucy, with this on her mind?

"It's just the strain of everything," she said. She would just have to have nerves of steel, and confront Aubrey later that night. Cade would probably stay over, given his current nervous state. She couldn't imagine him travelling back home alone. Jayne was certain there must be another explanation. Aubrey would provide it. He must.

26

It felt as if they were hunkering down amid a storm. Outside was the world of darkness, death, police, the winds of fear and suspicion and distrust. Inside: the strange stillness of the eye of the storm, peace, suspension from time.

With a fire lit, and candles, summer seemed long ago. They relied on Lucy for much of the early conversation. She was able to relate small and innocuous details about Amanda's family's movements that day, such as how long the police had spent with them, and what train they had returned on.

Cade said barely anything throughout the meal. Jayne could manage little more. Aubrey did his best. In the end the obvious thing was to acknowledge the tension.

"I'm quite sure this will go down in memory for all of us as the most joyless meal we have ever spent, on the saddest day. But I for one am glad to have your company with me on such a day," he said.

"It was very kind of you to invite us," Lucy said. "I know that I wouldn't have liked to be alone."

Aubrey offered all of them to stay over, as Jayne had suspected he would. Lucy declined as she had an early start the next day. "Otherwise I should have been very glad to do so, thank you."

Jayne was already staying at Aubrey's, and Cade's silence was taken as assent.

"Soon the police interviews will start, I expect," Aubrey said.

"What on earth shall we say?" Lucy asked.

"We can only answer their questions. When we last saw her, her state of mind, if she had mentioned anything unusual such as a jealous boyfriend."

Jayne remembered that Lucy did not know about Amanda's investigations. That was good, it made things easier for her at least. She hoped neither of the boys would bring it up now, in front of Lucy.

"There will of course be an inquest, and witnesses will be called. We must be prepared for that," Aubrey said.

Jayne had tried not to look at Aubrey too much during the meal, since her feelings were so conflicted. But now she found herself giving him a sharp glance. Was he suggesting they work on some sort of consistent statement between themselves?

Currently the police wouldn't have any reason to suspect a link between Amanda's murder and the attack on Cade. Let alone the death of Caroline and disappearance of Maria Tsakalotos, taking place as they did over a thousand miles away in Greece and not even considered suspicious. Jayne simply could not imagine how it would all play out if they tried to explain. The reaction might well be one of derision. Then there was another consideration: Amanda's family. And Caroline's of course, and Maria's.

A taxi had been called for Lucy, she had been seen safely away, and now the three of them sat together in front of the gas fire. Aubrey had made himself a hot milky drink he described as a posset, but the others declined to join him. "This is the twentieth century," Cade said. "People drink coffee and cocoa since the New World was discovered."

"So what do we do, then?" Jayne asked. "It's so fearsomely complicated."

Aubrey was silent for a moment, nursing his cup.

"What's interesting with Amanda's death is that it's the first time a murder has actually been identified," he said.

Caroline's death had been considered an accident. Maria's as a disappearance. The attempted murder on Cade was reported as a traffic accident. Whoever was responsible must be getting desperate, since they hadn't even attempted to try and make Amanda's murder look accidental.

"So this at last opens the possibility that someone might finally be brought to justice," Aubrey said.

Even if the only person it could practically be was Aubrey, Jayne thought.

She had to find out about the Delphinians leaflet. She must talk with him alone, later. Hopefully the posset wouldn't send him to sleep even sooner than Cade.

But Cade looked even more hollow. "It feels like ages have passed," he said. "It's as though all this happened years ago, and I can no longer remember a time before it, an untroubled time."

"You do look very tired, Cade. Why don't you turn in for the night?" Jayne said.

"I might just do that." He left them.

When he had gone, Jayne said: "I'm worried he's nearing a breakdown. What should we do?"

"He needs to get away from here," Aubrey said.

"To his mother's perhaps? Up north?"

"I fear if we send him up there he may hide away for months, years even. Somewhere warmer might do him good, particularly now the nights are starting to draw in here. The South of France perhaps. He hasn't been overseas for a while."

This was the perfect opening.

"Talking of which," Jayne began. There was no way to dress it up, so she just came out with it. She was too numb to try and find a tactful way to put the question, to give Aubrey an out. "When Cade and I were reading here earlier, a flyer dropped out of one of your books. For the Delphinians society." She looked at him as she said this, then looked down at her hands, waiting, willing him to speak and say that would defuse her fears.

Aubrey took some moments to respond. "I'd better not try and come up with something elaborate or fanciful, had I? Or deny ever seeing it."

"No. I think we're past all that."

"Of course. Well, I am afraid you have found me out. Not for the murders, of course not that, but for something that is shameful nonetheless. I should have told you, or I should have at least claimed knowledge of the society, but

I was foolish and afraid, which can only have resulted in your distrust."

"Oh Aubrey!" He sounded so contrite that Jayne felt a wave of guilt for even having found the leaflet.

"I have a bit of a weakness, I'm afraid. It's partly the thrill. Just having them. I'm lucky enough to be able to afford them, or perhaps it's unlucky? If I were poorer I mightn't be tempted. And I do keep the very greatest care of them."

"What exactly are you referring to, Aubrey?" said Jayne, confused.

"My collection. My artefacts." He got up and picked up a bronze statuette on the mantelpiece.

"I don't quite understand."

"I've acquired many of them through rather unorthodox means."

"You mean they're stolen?" Jayne asked.

"No, no not at all!" Aubrey was indignant. "It would just be difficult to buy and import them in a more conventional way."

"You mean they're smuggled?"

"I suppose one might put it like that."

"So how do the Delphinians come into all this?"

Aubrey set the bronze back on the shelf, adjusting its position carefully. "They help facilitate the purchase and transfer. They manage a sort of underground market, where one can make it known that one has a particular *objet* for sale, or that one is looking for such. I think of it as a sort of private network for collectors."

"That's not all the Delphinians do, is it?"

"That is my only involvement with them. I speak in all honesty."

"I rather imagine your involvement helps fund some of their other, even more dubious activities," Jayne said.

She looked at a nearby vase, a Grecian urn, black paint outlining warriors on ancient red clay. "So you mean to say that this isn't a replica, it's actually thousands of years old?"

Aubrey looked slightly offended. "None of my pieces are replicas! I suppose you couldn't be expected to know that though. I was rather anxious about Lucy. Would that she had stayed in mediaeval manuscripts, or whatever she was doing before. I have no interest in those."

"Lucy did seem quite surprised by them the other day. The centaur in your study in particular."

"She has discernment at least. That's my most valuable piece."

"So it is actually part of the Elgin marbles?"

"It was separated from the other panels hundreds of years ago and thought to be lost or destroyed. Well over a century before Lord Elgin collected the others. So technically I don't think one could describe it as an Elgin marble."

"It's still a Parthenon marble though. What would happen if someone found out about these?" Jayne asked.

"An international furore and I'd lose my job, I should imagine. Though it's not necessarily illegal, more of a grey area. Besides, did you know that the British Museum only has room to exhibit a fraction of its collection? Far too many artefacts are languishing in dusty museum basements all over the world. At least my pieces are out on display, and can be enjoyed."

It was too late for further discussion. They were both far too tired. Jayne was both relieved and troubled by Aubrey's explanation. She thought that it was his need to own these objects, considering the cost and risk, that worried her more than the actual illegality of it.

What had Amanda discovered? she wondered. And how had the culprit known? Could Amanda have tried to play a lone hand, perhaps ruffle some feathers? She had certainly been very angry about Caroline's death.

If only Amanda had phoned someone before leaving work. If only she hadn't walked out alone. If only they had never asked her to take on this foolish, dangerous task.

Who had known what she was doing? Who had needed her dead?

27

It was a grey day with foul, drizzling rain. They were all up late, and Mrs H already had breakfast ready. Jayne tried to eat a little, out of politeness.

Cade didn't even sit at the table. Instead he went to the window seat, and sat and stared at the bleak weather outside. He didn't even speak.

Aubrey ate his toast in silence, looking thoughtfully and worriedly at him. "There's something we didn't discuss yesterday, what with the shock, but it occurs to me that we may all be at risk. I think it wise for all of us - you, me, Cade and Lucy - to avoid being alone, and particularly walking about alone." He spoke in a lowered voice, to avoid Cade's ears.

"There must be an end to this soon. Now the police finally have something to go on," Jayne said.

Cade suddenly got up from the window and came to the table. He refused a chair and remained standing.

"This situation is driving me mad. This weather is driving me mad. I know you've both been talking about me, and think that I'm cracking up. Perhaps I am. I just know that I can't cope with it anymore and I have to get away."

"We did wonder about you staying with your mother for a while," Jayne said.

"Not there, not like this. I want to go to Greece."

"Greece?" Aubrey was incredulous.

"You've all been there. I want to see this place, the source of all this evil."

"Things happened there, but it was only an arena for them. It didn't cause them," Jayne said.

"Nonetheless, I shall buy myself a ticket today. I need to get away, and there's nowhere else to go. And you forget something. Caroline is still there, or her body. Someone must find her, and bring her home."

"Very well. Then we shall both accompany you," Aubrey said.

Jayne had feared that it might be too soon after Amanda's death to go overseas. But due to the circumstances, Amanda's parents planned a very private, family burial, not wanting any media attention. So there were fewer compelling reasons for any of them to stay around.

"We'll remember Amanda in our own way," Aubrey assured her. "As with Caroline, they may decide to hold a memorial for her later on, after the inquest is complete."

The mention of an inquest reminded Jayne of another grisly prospect. If everything linked up, it was increasingly likely that the body buried as Caroline would have to be exhumed. She could only imagine what that would be like for Caroline's parents.

"I'm not particularly religious," she said to Aubrey, "and I don't feel that there should be anything mystical about human remains. And yet the thought of that poor girl's bones lying so far from her home, and Caroline not properly laid to rest, also far from home, sickens me."

Aubrey was still of the mind that John was the likeliest suspect. "He's always had a ruthless streak. And you may be interested to learn that his mother was half Russian."

Jayne thought this was rather tenuous, but said nothing.

At first Cade would not speculate as to the perpetrator. Then he said: "Perhaps I have done Rory an injustice. Perhaps he is actually quite a brilliant actor, far better than me."

The night before they left, Aubrey held a final dinner, inviting both Lucy and Lucas.

They had finally decided to tell Lucy what they knew, including the issue of the second agent and their true fears regarding Caroline's death. Since there was no longer an understanding between her and John, it made certain suspicions less awkward. There had previously been a sense of wanting to protect her, even though in many ways Lucy was the most resilient of all.

It was a lot for anyone to take in. Lucy was silent for a long while. Then she said: "I need to think about all this more carefully. I knew John, you see, or at least I thought I did. So please give me some time to think it through."

Cade was noticeably improved. While he was still nervous to be left alone, and continued to stay with Aubrey and Jayne in Bloomsbury, something of his old self manifested from time to time. He was not too worried about work either, as the reviews for his play had been so stellar that he had been approached for several other productions, including a television series.

Lucy left first, and Aubrey and Cade tactfully went to bed early so Jayne could be alone with Lucas. She still had no clear idea where she stood with him, and was concerned that he had not mentioned anything regarding Victoria.

"He's obviously not the most devoted of fiancés is he?" Cade pointed out when they were alone in the kitchen for a moment. "Even setting aside his romantic overtures towards you, he barely seems to mention her."

Jayne thought that given the circumstances this was probably to be expected. Lucas was hardly likely to wax lyrical about Victoria's charms in front of her. Besides which everything between them had been so fast and fleeting, and so overshadowed by all the deaths.

Aubrey also allayed her concerns. "*Que sera sera.* From the way he looks at you his feelings are quite clear. A betrothal is dissolved as easily as it is made."

Jayne still felt unsure of things, and worried about the possible hurt to Victoria. Even though she had not particularly liked her, she did not wish her ill.

She sat with Lucas by the fire, wondering if he would raise the topic but he did not. Perhaps he felt it was more appropriate for him to speak with Victoria first, she thought.

She had decided not to tell Lucas about Cade and Harry. Cade remained very embarrassed about the liaison, and since his alibi absolved Harry from her earlier suspicions, there was no point raising it. She did however share Cade's list with him.

"I fear we've been too haphazard about this, perhaps because we've all been too fixated on our gut feelings and suspicions rather than the facts," Jayne said.

"Lucy must have better insight into John and his behaviour, including more accurate information about his overseas trips. Given they were engaged, as you say," Lucas said.

He was troubled by Jayne returning to Greece. "You were assaulted and threatened last time. They may employ someone less amateur than Yiannis on a future occasion. Urgent business keeps me here, unfortunately, or I should join you. But at least you won't be alone."

"Something about that whole episode still seems unreal," Jayne said. "I can't put my finger on it, but the more I think about it, the less in character it seems from what we know of the Delphinians. My questions, however clumsy, hardly seem worthy of their notice or concern. Someone must have been rattled though."

Lucas made her promise to call him if there was any trouble, or if she was worried even in the slightest about anything.

"It does feel like a kind of madness, the three of us making this trip," Jayne said. "But Cade was so determined. If only it helps him get stronger and gives us some resolution. I don't even know what we're looking for any more."

"It does seem absurdly complex. Which makes me wonder if it is in fact simple, and has been deliberately made to look complicated. But I can't yet see how or why."

28

As they flew out, Jayne felt unsure of the real reason for
their trip to Greece. Was it a mission, an escape, or a
recuperation? She mentioned this to Audrey while they
were boarding the plane.

"Whatever we do there depends on what this is, what
this is supposed to be," she said. "Do we charge around
investigating things? Will we sit around reminiscing about
lost friends?"

"What does it feel like to you?" Aubrey said.

Jayne considered for a moment. "I think that most of all
it feels like a pilgrimage."

"Then it is a pilgrimage," Aubrey said.

She realised that to each one of them it represented
something different. To Cade, it was an escape and even a
kind of holiday. He needed a change of scenery and he
needed to heal. To Aubrey it was partly a work trip, since
his job allowed him to combine leisure travel with
business. Jayne had first come here on holiday and
sighted Caroline, and she had been here a second time on

a quest to investigate her death. Now perhaps it was time to lay the ghost, and simply pay homage to Caroline for a third and final time.

Late September was still a hot month in the region, though the main tourist season was past. They had left London on a dry yet grey and windy day, and just a few hours later they were bathed in the warm afternoon sunshine of Athens.

Jayne booked the hillside villa that she had first stayed in with her cousins. It was available, and at a cheaper rate, due to now being off-season. She thought it wiser to avoid staying in the Villa Kallina a second time, as well as wiser to stay outside the town.

They left the airport, a taxi was arranged, and by early evening they had arrived at the villa.

It was starting to seem a familiar route to Jayne; she had made this journey three times now. Arriving at the villa again in different company made her feel rather like the hostess, and she found herself arranging and assigning the bedrooms. It felt like her turn as well, she had stayed at both Cade's and Aubrey's places, and now they stayed at her villa.

Cade had a renewed energy that was verging on manic. He couldn't sit still, he wanted to go down to the town immediately to see the harbour, then he wanted to see Delphi by night.

"It would just be totally dark there, there would be nothing to see," Jayne told him. "We can go tomorrow."

She felt cast in the role of tour guide as they all went out to find somewhere to eat. Used to having Cade and Aubrey squabble over restaurant recommendations, now they sought her suggestions. This at least allowed her to deliberately avoid the places she had frequented before. If Cade wanted to visit the spot where she had seen Caroline, he could do so tomorrow.

They ate in a small restaurant in a side street that Jayne had not been to before. She had liked the look of it, but her cousins had always dragged her to the waterfront. Apart from one elderly couple across the room, the three of them were the only diners in there.

We're all waiting for something, Jayne thought. But for what, or whom?

Cade got very drunk on ouzo and had to be helped home. Normally this would have been an annoyance, but it was a relief having something to occupy herself with.

With Cade in bed, Jayne and Aubrey sat alone in the small courtyard in the still-balmy night air, woven with jasmine. Jayne was aware that voices carried through the walls very easily. She had been disturbed from sleep a few times during her first stay, so she tried to keep her voice low.

Jayne had kept Aubrey's secret, not even telling Cade, though she feared that Lucy already knew something was amiss with Aubrey's collection. So long as Aubrey didn't attempt to secure further artefacts on this trip, his methods of collection were not directly relevant to their mission. His knowledge of the Delphinians may or may not be an advantage.

"So what do we do from here?" she asked Aubrey.

"Our number one priority would appear to be keeping an eye on the boy Francis, that's clear."

Aubrey was not without experience in this area, having roomed with Cade during their university days.

Aubrey's plan was to try and identify the mysterious "Englishman" who had been seen with Maria in the time leading up to her disappearance. He was armed with several photographs of John and Rory.

"I've started to wondering whether there may be two cases here, and perhaps it doesn't all link up at all," Jayne said. "When Caroline first died we didn't even think it was murder, and we certainly didn't have any motives in mind. Now there's the whole espionage affair, and yet there are still more holes than there are correlations.

"Could Maria's death have genuinely been an accident? Or might Caroline be the one who deliberately switched identities? If she was working with Maria, she would have known about her death. Perhaps she swapped their papers around so she could track down who killed Maria? When I saw Caroline, and she didn't answer, maybe that was because she was trying to impersonate Maria?"

"The difficulty with that is Caroline's family being informed of her death. I fear that she would not have let things go so far. You saw her even after Harry had already had time to make the various arrangements," Aubrey said.

"I have wondered about that. Including the procedure by which it happens, how they notify relatives, and how quickly it happens. I thought about that when Amanda died, the process of it all. With her family it was within a couple of hours."

"For deaths overseas I believe the local police, having found a foreign passport, would notify the respective embassy, in this instance the British Embassy in Athens.

The Embassy would notify the Foreign Office, who then notify the local UK police, who then notify the next of kin," Aubrey said.

"It's quite a few steps then. They must have to be fairly efficient to get the news delivered quickly."

"Such matters would be handled as a priority. Our question is really whether the identity mix-up was accidental or deliberate. And if it was deliberate was it carried out by Caroline herself or by the killer? If the latter, then why?"

As promised, the next morning they took Cade to Delphi. He seemed to enjoy it, wandering off among the ruins. Aubrey had of course been there before.

"The Delphinians throw some rather bacchanalian parties here," he said. "But of course you know about that."

"Yes. Dancing in the stadium and wine cellars in the shrines. Quite a convenient location."

"For other things too," Aubrey said, looking rather shamefaced.

"Oh Aubrey! You don't mean this is where you come to do your shady deals?"

"Sometimes. It depends what it is. Too many eyes in the town. And the shrine vaults make such a safe hidey-hole."

Cade came back over to them. Jayne was happy to see more of a spring in his step. "The views here are superb, but I could use a coffee. Are there any cafés?" he asked.

"None on site, but we can go into Delphi town. There's the Archaeological Museum there too."

"I suppose I should do the full sightseeing thing. It might even give me a heightened appreciation for Aubrey's knick-knacks."

Jayne noticed Aubrey wince, though whether from guilt or pain at the insult to his collection she couldn't tell.

She had greatly admired the statue of the Charioteer when she had seen it the first time during her holiday with her cousins. Now as she stood looking at it again, it was unsettlingly familiar. Aubrey gazed upon it covetously.

"It's far too big for even your flat," Jayne said. "Besides which you couldn't sit around with that staring at you every day. I don't know why I didn't see it before, but it looks very like Cade."

"Yes," Aubrey said. His single word managed to tell Jayne everything that could be said. How had she never realised before?

She didn't know what to say. Anything would have sounded trite in the circumstances. No wonder he had been so silent after Cade revealed his situation with Harry.

Cade, oblivious, came over to the statue. "How splendid. And how very attractive."

"We were just remarking that it rather looks like you," Jayne said.

"Do you know I think it does." He was very pleased with the idea.

After Delphi they had lunch, then split up for the afternoon. Aubrey trotted off to the Delphinians' office for some further investigations. Cade wanted to go for a walk along the sea. Jayne decided to look up Yiannis.

But when she arrived at the bar, he was nowhere to be found. "He doesn't work here anymore," one of the other waiters told her. "He went to Athens some weeks ago."

Uncertain if she should be concerned, Jayne asked if they had heard from him. Fortunately she was told that Yiannis was back regularly as he had a girl in the town. He had gone to Athens to earn more money as he wanted to marry her.

That was one fear eased at least. Jayne was deciding whether to stay for a drink or wander back along the harbour front when something stopped her.

At the end of the room, at a small table, sat John.

Her first reaction was fear. If he was here it could only mean one thing. She had known it had to be him or Rory. The transition from a rather cold, bookish man that she disliked to someone who had arranged Caroline's death and murdered Amanda was still hard to contemplate.

We knew there was one of us that betrayed the others, Jayne thought. The snake in the grass. The serpent in Arcadia. And here he was, finally.

John had gone to Caroline's funeral and feigned condolences for a death he had carried out. He had attended the memorial and even used it as an opportunity to threaten and intimidate.

There he was, reading a newspaper. Something in his calm and sedate manner infuriated Jayne and turned her chill of fear to an icy anger. She went up to him and confronted him.

"How could you do this? What could possibly be worth it? Did you really think that their lives were worth so much less than yours? Caroline, Cade, Amanda?"

John looked up, startled.

"Jayne, why are you saying this to me?"

"How can you just sit there? You will never get away with this. Even if you run out now you won't escape, they will find you. I can't believe I didn't just go to the police weeks ago. How stupidly timid, how stupidly cautious we've all been!"

He stopped her.

"You've got it entirely wrong. It's not me. I'm here for the same reason you are."

29

"Before I even address the absurdity of your accusations let me just place a few facts before you," John said.

"First, I have an alibi for the time that Caroline was killed. I was overseas, but at a conference in Brussels. I have several colleagues who can confirm this. Secondly, I spent the entire night Amanda was killed in the company of a senior member of the judiciary. Thirdly, though perhaps I should have ordered these points chronologically, I was at home with my mother on the evening of Cade's accident.

"And on that latter point: we have as yet no evidence, nor do I even have any belief nor reason to believe, that Cade's accident was anything other than an unfortunate traffic mishap," John said.

"But you told me..." Jayne began.

"I merely told you that Cade's meddling in matters beyond his scope of concern risked putting lives at risk. Which it did. Intelligence operations are highly sensitive and his blundering about was disruptive."

His manner softened slightly, and he asked Jayne to sit down.

"Up to a point I partly blame myself," John said. "After all I was the one with the closest relationship and I should have realised earlier. But it is impossible to imagine that events would go this far. I was quite satisfied that Caroline's death was an accident, even after your absurd claim at the funeral. But now the motive is apparent, it clearly cannot be."

"When did you know?" Jayne felt deep regret that it must be Rory. She had to admit to herself that she had rather hoped it was John, since she disliked him.

"Immediately after Amanda was killed. There was no avoiding the issue then, since it couldn't be attributed to any natural or accidental cause."

John is so clinical, thought Jayne. It's as if he hides all human feelings behind cold logic. No wonder Lucy went cool on him.

As if he read her mind, John said: "Your problem is that you've gone about this the entirely wrong way. You dash off to Greece on a whim, without stopping to verify a single fact or figure."

"Actually this trip was Cade's idea. Its purpose was more recuperative than anything."

"I am not referring to this occasion. I mean your previous escapade. Had you thought to merely establish alibis before you went, you would have saved yourself considerable time and trouble. This entire matter simply comes down to alibis, and the need for them."

Jayne wasn't sure if she entirely followed. "So what do you plan to do?" she said.

"It's too late to do much, the damage is done. And I don't know if I have any influence, or whether it would be best to wait for the police to step in. But for the sake of former days and former friendships, all our friendships," his voice broke slightly, the first and only time Jayne would ever hear his composure falter, "I must do what I can."

He folded his newspaper.

"It is a very chastening thing, to think that one has known and admired another person for so long, and to have shared such intimate confidences with them, to then be so utterly deceived in their character."

Jayne was moved by his honesty. She knew that he and Rory had been very good friends, but she had not appreciated the strength of John's regard for him. No wonder he had struggled to accept the non-accidental causes of death.

"I don't think you are bound any further by the bonds of loyalty, John. We have all suffered enough."

John nodded, and left.

She lay there in the dark, with the flicker of a citronella candle casting strange shadows on the wall, and the endless ringing of crickets. Far away she could hear the faint thump of music; someone must be having a party. Jayne was reminded of the night she had been to Delphi with Lucas, and Yiannis's bizarre abduction of her. The rubble of the ruined temple or shrine, whatever it was. A treasury?

It felt strange to have finally handed everything over to someone else. Since Lucas's request, it had felt like her personal responsibility to see this through. And now John would handle the final denouement and deal with Rory and see matters brought to a close.

Or would he? What if Rory fled across the Iron Curtain at the last minute? What if he never confessed, and they were never able to find Caroline? Maria's bones were lying in Caroline's grave, so where did Caroline lie?

And then she sat up, because she suddenly had an idea where Caroline might be. Even more strongly, she felt a burning need to find out then and there. But it was past midnight, Cade and Francis were both asleep, and hailing a taxi at this hour would be near to impossible. She would have to wait until morning.

She slept fitfully and woke shortly before dawn. It was still far too early to wake the others. Even if she did drag them slowly, grumbling, from their beds they would still take ages to get ready. As she was only planning to take a look, she may as well go alone.

Jayne slipped on a pair of trousers and her shoes, and headed for the road. It didn't take long to see a taxi heading towards the town; local drivers started their shift around his time.

"To Delphi, please," she said.

It was not unusual for tourists to want to see sites at quieter times, often to take photographs uninterrupted by other visitors, so the driver showed no surprise or curiosity. He transported Jayne to her destination, took her drachmas, and drove back off.

She had seen Delphi by day and by night, and now she saw it at dawn. She was the first person here today; at least she could see no others around.

Somehow she had forgotten the size of the place, and how many small treasuries and ruined shrines lined the path zigzagging up the hillside. Her idea suddenly seemed rather more wild and speculative. But she persisted.

Jayne had remembered how crates of wine were stored in the cool cellar beneath one of the larger, better restored temples near the summit. But what if other little shrines also had vaults and storage places? They were treasuries after all. It would be such an easy, convenient place to put a body. No need to dig a shallow grave, or risk it washing ashore somewhere. Instead, store it in the earth, leave it be.

She wasn't quite sure what she was looking for, but even if she could narrow it down that might help. Several of the temples clearly didn't have basements, others seemed to have been undisturbed for years.

As she stumbled around the ruins, picking her way between the shrines, she had the odd sense that someone was watching her. But whenever she looked there was no one there. The sky had grown fully light now, and it looked like being another warm and sunny day.

And then, just as she found herself in a small temple with a flat stone floor that looked more promising - or would have done so if she had managed to take a crowbar along - she saw a figure approaching. And froze in shock.

It was Rory.

She would have known him a mile off. The way he slightly stooped due to his height, as though he was entering a doorway that was a couple of inches too short.

Why was he here? Hadn't John managed to speak with him? Surely he knew the game was up.

Rory's size, which had once seemed strong and attractive, now seemed lumbering and menacing. He was making his way over to her. Should she run? Should she grab a rock?

"Jayne!" he cried out.

She turned to try and escape, catching her foot on a piece of fallen masonry and twisting it painfully. It's too late, she thought, I've trapped myself here.

"Wait!"

Then as he neared, and she could see the detail of his face: his freckled complexion, the grim set to his mouth - she heard a loud crack and Rory suddenly buckled and fell. He didn't even cry out.

For a split second she was confused, then relieved, then terror struck her anew when she saw the figure who emerged from behind him.

There, clutching a gun, her face twisted with hate, was Lucy.

30

For a moment Jayne thought Lucy had shot Rory in her defence. That hope vanished when Lucy pointed the gun towards Jayne.

"Your turn next," Lucy said in her sweet, slightly high voice.

Her tone chilled Jayne far more than if she had shouted or snarled.

"What's going on? What have you done to Rory? We need to get him help!" Jayne said.

"I should say he's beyond that."

Am I hallucinating? thought Jayne. The morning sun was now shining bright across the ruins, the brilliant, unearthly light of daybreak. Lucy's shadow stretched across from her, long and thin.

"Please put the gun down, tell me what is going on?"

"You're so blind Jayne, you bumble around for months and have no idea about anything. I told Harry he didn't need to worry and he should have kept his mouth shut, but he panicked, and now things are too messy."

"Harry is involved in this? What about Rory?"

Lucy laughed. "All this time and these flits to Greece and back and you still have no idea, do you? But then you've never had any idea about anything, any of you."

"I'm afraid I don't understand what you mean."

"You're all so comfortable, aren't you, with your lovely houses and your independent wealth. You have no idea what it's like to actually need to work for what you have. Aubrey rattling around in his million dollar flat, wasting hundreds of thousands of pounds on smuggled stones and jars. Oh yes, I know about that. As if I'm so stupid that I can't distinguish between replicas and the real deal, given the dozens of items I deal with every week. And you, with your house and your endless comfortable leisure. And Caroline with an entire mansion coming to her, wanting to fill it with invalids and cripples! As if Harry was going to let her ruin it, to waste his rightful inheritance on something like that."

Harry and Lucy. The hideous realisation was dawning. Desperately Jayne thought back to her conversation with John. He had talked of close relationships, intimate confidences, admiration. *But he had never spoken a name.* How had she failed to realise that he was speaking of Lucy, not Rory?

"You mean you and Harry killed Caroline?"

"It was so humiliating for him, having to give it all up to a sister. That's not the traditional way of things at all. He carried the family name, it should have been his. And mine. And now it will be," Lucy smiled. She looked eerily sweet amid what could only be madness.

"You did all this for the house? You and Harry together?"

Lucy was getting impatient. "I was tired of never having anything. Even Amanda's parents are as rich as Croesus so she doesn't have to pay her own rent. And John was dragging his heels over the engagement, and I could see he was cooling off. And then I got talking with Harry one day at a party. He was going to end up with nothing as well, and he was just as fed up about it as I was. So it all fell into place. It took some time to arrange everything, but it was worth it.

"Now Caroline's dead, it's all ours. Once we marry." She saw Jayne's bewilderment. "And before you ask, Harry's little liaison with Cade was purely strategic. Harry needed an alibi, and he got an absolutely water-tight one, didn't he? That worked so beautifully. We didn't trust Victoria to be much use you see, she was starting to get annoying. She served her purpose well enough though. None of you had any idea about Harry and me, did you?"

She smiled again. Jayne's head was spinning amid her fear.

"I'm sorry Lucy, I don't understand. What do you mean about Victoria?"

"Harry pretending to be engaged to her. It was a brilliant front."

"But Victoria is engaged to Lucas."

For the first time Lucy's smile faltered. "Where on earth would you get that idea? She's engaged to Harry. Or she thinks she is. That was my idea."

It is said that your life flashes before your eyes when you are drowning. Now, as she crouched against a broken pillar not knowing when Lucy would pull the trigger, Jayne had flashbacks of all the times she had spent with

Lucas. Who was it who had first told her about Victoria and him?

Of course! It was Cade who mentioned it, at the funeral. He had overheard that Victoria was Lucas's fiancée. Or had he misheard? Had Victoria said something to the effect of "I'm the fiancée" while standing near both cousins? Given the situation between Cade and Harry, it might be natural for him to assume that Lucas was the person indicated.

For Jayne it also explained why Lucas never seemed to have any compunction about going out with her, dancing with her, even kissing her - and why he never mentioned Victoria.

But what about Harry? Hadn't he also confirmed the relationship? Jayne thought back to exactly what he had said during his bizarre confession, now finally unveiled as a tissue of lies. Yes, he had been surprised when Jayne mentioned Victoria, hadn't he? And even then Jayne had only referred to "the engagement", as though it was an isolated, external thing.

Harry had either realised that Jayne mistakenly understood Victoria and Lucas to be together, and had deliberately used that to his own advantage. Or he had thought that Jayne meant the news of any engagement would be upsetting to someone suffering heartbreak, albeit a heartbreak that he had entirely invented.

She must keep Lucy talking. Maybe someone would come.

"What about Amanda?"

"You all thought it was because she was meddling with government files, didn't you? Too funny! Unfortunately she found out about Harry and me. That was Harry's fault again. And she started asking questions, and it got awkward. I was worried she might tell you and you might finally join the dots. And now here I am telling you anyway! But it doesn't matter, because you'll be with Caroline soon. You and Rory. Safely tucked away where no one will ever find either of you."

"So it is Maria Tsakalotos who is buried in Caroline's grave then?" Jayne asked.

"The Greek girl, yes. That was such a brilliant plan. Except you ruined it of course, seeing Caroline when you weren't supposed to. I saw you earlier that week, you know, when you were with your cousins. You were all off sailing while I was there to kill Maria. But you didn't see me."

"Why Maria?" Oh if only someone would come, there must be other tourists arriving by now.

"She fitted Caroline's description. Harry gave me one of Caroline's old passports to plant on her body. It was quite easy. I put something in her drink, and pushed her off a boat. Harry was the only person who benefitted from Caroline's death, and he had the perfect alibi since he was with Cade the very night Caroline was supposed to have died. All according to our plan. And then you messed it all up by seeing Caroline a week later. So Harry panicked and came to you with that idiotic explanation. I warned him not to. The whole point was to keep everything as simple as possible."

Lucy frowned as she continued. "And Caroline didn't even speak with you, did she? She wasn't there as Caroline of course, that's why. She was in some silly disguise for one of her missions. So we could easily have got away with it and bluffed it out, but Harry lost his nerve. Getting that Greek fellow to put the wind up your sails was clever though. Harry pretended he was from the Delphinians. We thought that even if you weren't scared off, and I never thought you would be, at least you'd be confused."

"And what about Cade? Which one of you ran him over?"

"Neither of us," Lucy said. "I don't even drive, if you remember. That was just an accident, a very lucky accident as it turned out, since it helped confuse things even more for you all. We were also lucky with all those espionage rumours, weren't we? When you disappear everyone will think that you stirred the wrong hornet's nest and got bumped off by the Bulgarians. Rory too. It's so conveniently risky, his work. Or they may think he's fled to Russia thanks to all the rumours. How ironic that you should all have suspected him anyway. And most useful."

"So all of this - all these deaths - it was just so you and Harry could inherit the house?"

"We have such big plans for it. We'll need money of course, which is where the Delphinians and my job come in so useful. Aubrey is nearly singlehandedly bankrolling our plans, unbeknownst to him. Harry's going to put in a golf course and a casino and convert a wing to luxury flats. Rich Russians and Americans will snap them up."

"But if you do this, Lucy, everyone will know. They'll find out you were here."

"Oh that's fine, since John's here. It was me who tipped him off about you coming. I shall simply go and have a big scene with him later today, and beg him to take me back, and he'll refuse, and I'll fly back heartbroken and claim he was my sole reason for coming. Everyone's so used to pathetic little Lucy that they'll just feel sorry for me."

Actually we don't think of you like that, Jayne thought. Everyone has always seen Lucy as sweet but spirited, even resilient. It was only now that Lucy seemed pathetic: the obsession, the jealousy, the murderous mania.

"Lucas will work it out though. He's already suspicious of Harry," Jayne warned her.

"Oh that tedious cousin, always on Harry's back. I expect he'll be heartbroken when you vanish. Perhaps he and Victoria can console one another, how apt that would be, since you already thought they were an item!" Lucy laughed. "We'll just cook him the wrong kind of mushrooms or something if he starts any trouble. There are so many ways. It's easier once you've done it once, you learn from your mistakes."

Lucy pointed the gun more directly, and there was a click.

Jayne heard a shout, and out of the corner of her eye thought she saw a figure running.

But then there was a crack. A sudden jolt, as though she had been punched.

An eternity of numbness when the world seemed to stand still.

Then a white hot burning and blackness.

31

The first thing she became aware of was how perfect the warmth of the blanket was. So light, and yet so warm. She never wanted it to be moved off her. Was she sleeping? Who had put it there? It wasn't her usual blanket.

She started to open her eyes, but it seemed so bright in the room and she wanted to sleep longer. She closed them again.

"Jayne."

It was his voice. She thought she had dreamt about him, but she wasn't sure.

"I'm so tired. So heavy." She couldn't seem to move.

"Everything's alright, you're safe. Just sleep." She felt a hand on her brow. "We won't leave you."

She drifted off again.

When she woke again the light was much dimmer. There was a hot, dull ache all over her left side. Something was stuck to her right arm and she tried to raise it but she had no power.

"Don't move your arm, stay still, I'll fetch a nurse." A nurse? Was she in hospital?

Half an hour later she had been shifted and checked and prodded and poked by nurses and a doctor, and she knew that she was in a hospital in Athens, and that she had been shot. According to the doctors it was a miracle that the bullet had missed doing more extensive damage. Lucas, Cade and Aubrey were all by her bedside.

"You lost a lot of blood. If the bullet had been just a fraction of an inch further across you probably wouldn't have made it. At least we can now compare near death experiences. Did you find yourself going down a tunnel with a bright light at the end?" That was Cade.

Bits and pieces were coming back to Jayne. The ruins. Lucy. The morning sunlight. A gun catching the light.

Lucy! "Where's Lucy?" she asked.

"She's with the police." It was Lucas who answered.

"Did she say what happened?"

"All we know is that she shot you. She wouldn't say anything after that. John's sorting out what he can for her, more for her parents' sake I believe. There's not a lot that can be done but he's trying to arrange decent legal representation."

"What about Rory? He was there, wasn't he?"

The look on their faces told them all she needed to know. She closed her eyes again, as tears filled them.

It turned out that Cade had possibly been Jayne's saviour. He had woken early and seen her bedroom door open, but no trace of her.

"I didn't think you had been kidnapped, but it seemed unusually impulsive for you, and it gave me a bad feeling. I woke Aubrey, and we had to decide where to look for you. He went down to the town while I headed the other way to Delphi. When I got there I saw you and Lucy from a distance, and then when I got closer I saw what was happening. I yelled, but she fired. She would have shot you again but I wrestled with her for the gun. By then there were some other people around who went for an ambulance. It was too late for Rory, her aim was deadlier the first time. It must have been pretty instant, he wouldn't have suffered."

"I remember everything up to the gunshot, I think," Jayne said. "I do remember thinking there was a figure, but the sun was in my eyes, or it was gleaming off the gun - everything goes rather hazy there."

Piece by piece, she told them what Lucy had said. "We were totally on the wrong track. I did have my doubts about Harry that one time, but then he had that perfect alibi. And who would have thought of Lucy? All those years she was secretly resenting us. She was our friend, and she hated us enough to kill us."

Aubrey and Cade tactfully made an exit, leaving Jayne alone with Lucas.

"You were here earlier weren't you? I remember someone speaking to me when it was still light. How did you get here so quickly?" she asked.

"You do realise a whole day has passed, don't you?"

Jayne had not realised. "So it all happened yesterday not this morning? I can't believe I slept for so long."

"You nearly died of blood loss. You were in surgery for several hours."

"It's very disorientating, waking on the wrong day. It gives me a better appreciation for what Cade went through. He was out for over ten days. No wonder he's been struggling since."

Lucas sat by the bed and took her hand. "Thank god you are alive. I don't know what I should have done if I'd landed in Athens to be told the worst. The flight was hard enough, not knowing for all those hours."

Jayne smiled up at him. "I am very glad you're here." Then she remembered what Lucy had revealed about Lucas, and a flicker of embarrassment passed over her.

"What's wrong?" Lucas asked. Jayne explained Cade's mistake and her own assumptions. "Good god, you thought that I was engaged to Victoria! My behaviour must have looked irredeemably caddish."

"Mine was even more inexcusable, given I actually believed you were otherwise involved."

Lucas laughed. "I'm glad your better nature didn't manage to keep me at arm's length. Though we might have cleared this up earlier if you had tried to."

"That poor girl. It will be awful for her when they arrest Harry," Jayne said. "She knows nothing about any of this, and all the revelations that must come out will be very difficult for her."

"I should think she'll survive," Lucas said drily. "She had barely known Harry before their engagement, and I suspect the whirlwind romance was more to do with a landed title than my cousin's personal charms."

They were both silent. Jayne thought of Caroline's and Harry's parents. They had been devastated enough by Caroline's death. How would they cope now?

Exhaustion flooded her. As she slipped back to sleep, she felt Lucas kiss her forehead.

Jayne was in hospital for over a week, and it was another week before the doctors deemed it safe for her to travel.

Cade, Aubrey and Lucas remained in Greece to be with her. They talked over everything, every detail, wondering how they had failed to ever suspect Lucy. "I did give her a silver star," Cade said, but Jayne pointed out that it was barely in earnest, and the motive was entirely wrong.

"It's thinking of her all those years, resenting us. Appearing so bright and happy, yet filled with hate and envy," Jayne said.

"Perhaps she was happy then. People change. It may have been later that it started. University life can be so unreal. Everyone is artificially on a level: the same accommodation, the same meals, the same tutorials. When you leave, things restratify," Lucas said.

"She was doing very well for herself though, with her job, wasn't she?"

"She was, but that profession is not particularly highly paid," Aubrey said.

Lucy was so pretty, thought Jayne. Is, she reminded herself. They found themselves talking about her as though she was dead. Why couldn't she just have married money? If not John, then there were hundreds of other eligible men that didn't need to commit fratricide to comfortably provide for her.

It was about hate too, she thought, not solely money. Two people angry at a world in which they felt denied.

"So the other agent was Rory all along. It should have been obvious really. And he must have been the English friend of Maria Tsakalotos. If only we'd considered bringing him into our confidence from the start, all this might have been avoided," Jayne said. She bitterly regretted dismissing Rory's offer of help.

"You can't blame yourself," Cade said. "If we had done so, they might have tried to take him out earlier. They were increasingly ruthless and desperate."

And for nothing really, Jayne thought. For a house that although beautiful, haemorrhaged money. Lucy could have become so much richer simply through the smuggling racket. But that would not have brought the status which she felt she was owed.

"I think back to all the times I spoke with Lucy over the past weeks, and can't stop agonising over things I must have missed. Should it have been more obvious? I fear that I've too often heard what I wanted to hear, rather than really listened to what people are actually saying," Jayne said. She remembered her conversations with Harry and John with some pain.

"Even if Amanda had lived to tell me about Lucy and Harry, would I have realised the implications? Did Amanda herself realise? Or would the two of them have been able to spin further lies?"

"We will never know," Lucas said. "At the end of the day you did what you could. We all did."

"It was unprecedented evil," said Aubrey. In some ways he was the most shaken of all of them, Jayne thought. She had not repeated Lucy's jeer that Aubrey was effectively funding their plans, but she knew he felt both foolish and culpable for his albeit unknowing role.

32

The garden was frosty that morning. It was late November now and Jayne was nearly back to full strength. The doctors had told her that she was lucky to have kept the use of her arm.

The distressing process of exhuming Caroline's grave had been carried out and as expected, dental records had proven the body to be that of Maria Tsakalotos. The Greek woman's grieving family reburied her in a small cemetery in Patras. Jayne had written to them. She had never met Maria, but there would always be a connection.

They had found Caroline's body near to where Jayne had guessed it might be, and flown her remains back home. It was little consolation for her parents, given their new grief over finding out their own son had killed her.

There was a memorial for Amanda, and a funeral for Rory. Just the four of them remained now, with Lucy in prison, awaiting trial, along with Harry.

Cade had fully recovered. He was slightly piqued to learn that his accident was just that, a coincidence rather than a conspiracy to kill. But it also erased the last vestiges of his fear. He was back on the stage again, and getting rave reviews.

Aubrey had faithfully promised Jayne to keep to more orthodox channels when making any future transactions. In return he had made her promise to stay with him whenever she was in London. He had enjoyed her company more than he had expected, and his vast flat now seemed very empty without guests.

John had returned to his chambers. They didn't expect to see a great deal of him in future. His engagement with Lucy and his friendship with Rory had been the main glue keeping him in contact with them, and now these things were gone forever. They had had little in common with him at university; there were even fewer links now.

And then there was Lucas. Here now, in the bare and wintry garden, telling her something she had hoped to hear for so long.

"I know it's soon, but after all the death and pointless loss, life just seems more precious. I first fell in love with you here, even though I barely knew you, and after all we have been through I know that my feelings won't change," he said. "Will you marry me?"

To marry him would be wonderful. Yet it would also be easy. Over the past months Jayne had vowed to herself that she needed to live more than merely exist. To do rather than drift. Amanda's accusation of retirement had been fair, and out of respect to her friend, she had decided to address it.

"I would like to very much, but I would also like to wait," she said. Recovering from her injury had given her time to think about her future plans, though she hadn't shared them with anyone yet, even Cade.

"I'm planning to take a course in horticulture. Then I'd like to work on the gardens at the new convalescent home, if there's a job for me there."

Lucas had discussed Caroline's plans with her parents, and they had decided to implement them in tribute to her. The convalescent home would be named in Caroline's memory. It was going to be a major project. An entire wing of the house would be redeveloped, as well as several acres of ground that had been badly neglected in recent years due to cost and time.

"Of course there will be," Lucas said. "But I would rather have you there as my wife than my employee."

He had tentatively agreed to run the place for his aunt and uncle. There was also the unspoken knowledge that he would likely inherit in place of his cousin, depending on the intricacies of entail law and forfeiture.

"I will wait then. I don't suppose you would like to at least move in with me first?"

"To start with, I'm moving into Amanda's old flat. I'm taking the rest of her lease. I should be able to afford it if I let this place out. So I'll be nearby, and then we can see," Jayne said.

He answered her without words, his lips warm in the cold winter air. She felt simultaneously safe and terrified with him.

As he held her, she looked over the bare trees and the dormant beds, awaiting spring. Jayne knew that she was leaving her Eden, casting herself out, though she could always return. But somehow she doubted that she ever would.

About Edward Turbeville

Edward Turbeville is a mystery writer from England's ancient Forest of Dean.

His favourite authors include Agatha Christie, Evelyn Waugh, P G Wodehouse and Nevil Shute.

Edward is also a fan of the Classics, notably Cicero and Vergil, and has published and alliterative verse translation of Book III of the Aeneid.

His website is: **http://www.edwardturbeville.com**

You can also sign up for Edward's mailing list at: **http://www.subscribepage.com/edward**

Lightning Source UK Ltd.
Milton Keynes UK
UKOW05f1241201016

285747UK00002B/7/P